“Father Rock is an action packed original book and film concept developed by T. R. Brooks to appeal to a world-wide audience. It is a classic good versus evil tale with a unique twist. The story culminates in the ultimate battle for world dominance in which the main characters do battle with musical weapons.

Father Rock is a white-haired wizard god with a laser light guitar. Demos is the subterranean fire-breathing monster. The basic story is designed to touch on all the human emotions. It is an intelligent concept conveyed in the American music style. Which combines the best of the European epic tale with the American appetite for action and adventure.

I believe it has the potential to be a classic; a new Fantasia or Dante's Inferno.”

Ralph G. DePalma, III
Entertainment Attorney
New York

“Father Rock is a spellbinding and truly original work. While the story is certainly a great literary adventure, it speaks much of our esoteric nature, cosmic forces around us, and the path we all must take towards our higher nature.” - Steve Mundahl, publisher, Lifestyles/Circe Press

FATHER ROCK

T.R. Brooks

Order this book online at www.trafford.com/06-2333
or email orders@trafford.com

Most Trafford titles are also available at major online book retailers.

Note for Librarians: A cataloguing record for this book is available from Library and Archives Canada at www.collectionscanada.ca/amicus/index-e.html

ISBN: 978-1-4251-0575-4

We at Trafford believe that it is the responsibility of us all, as both individuals and corporations, to make choices that are environmentally and socially sound. You, in turn, are supporting this responsible conduct each time you purchase a Trafford book, or make use of our publishing services. To find out how you are helping, please visit www.trafford.com/responsiblepublishing.html

Our mission is to efficiently provide the world's finest, most comprehensive book publishing service, enabling every author to experience success. To find out how to publish your book, your way, and have it available worldwide, visit us online at www.trafford.com/10510

www.trafford.com

North America & international
toll-free: 1 888 232 4444 (USA & Canada)
phone: 250 383 6864 • fax: 250 383 6804
email: info@trafford.com

The United Kingdom & Europe
phone: +44 (0)1865 722 113 • local rate: 0845 230 9601
facsimile: +44 (0)1865 722 868 • email: info.uk@trafford.com

10 9 8 7 6 5 4 3

I would like to dedicate this book to Paul Calamia. A gifted young guitarist / singer / songwriter who is fighting lung cancer. He is a good friend and a great talent.

Paul Calamia

Many thanks to all the people who helped me along the way. Especially my wife Debbie Brooks, Mike, Aura, Austen, Chad, and Logan. Thank you to my family for their infinite love and patience during the creation of this book.

I would like to add special thanks to, William E .Parramore (a.k.a.Wild Bill), Nadine Speller, John Fok, and Gary Blythe.

Also thanks to Patrick Ernst and Sherry Smith Gray (a.k.a. sherisaid), for editing and helping me refine and develop the writing in this book. To Sandy Maroon for those final finishing touches. Also Darren Summers for his great illustrations and hard work on the cover.

- T.R. Brooks

Map of Galtor Region
Red Crystal Range
Dragon Top
Black Crystal Mountain
Demo's Cave
Death Swamp
Dragon Land
Father Rock's Home
Blue Crystal Run
River of Death
Demon's Henge
River of Life
Valley of Demons
Snake Lake
the Swamp of Demons

Prologue

Robert sees himself and his friend Bill playing ball in the park. Next to the park is a graveyard. They are on the same football team. Robert is the quarterback for Middletown High School. He has great potential as a professional football player. Bill is a troublesome type of boy, constantly in hot water with the police and on probation for breaking and entering. Robert is a very good influence on Bill. Bill passes the ball and it goes far too high and over a bush. The bush is very thick and Robert has to break limbs to get through a thick maze of growth. He moves a branch and sees a stone entryway. On the entryway walls are very strange looking symbols and his curiosity takes over.

He starts to crawl into the cave-like entryway but it soon becomes too dark to see. As he moves his right hand, he hits something. The object is oblong and partially buried in the ground. He digs it free. It turns out to be a metal box with an odd-looking symbol on top. He does not try to open the box. He carries it out in the sunlight, so Bill can also be there for the opening. Robert's heart beats fast and his hands sweat. What could this be? The black box looks very old with strange writing all over it. This could be almost anything, but one thing for sure: it is exciting, very exciting.

Robert yells, "Bill, wait till you see what I found. It's unbelievable. It looks like it's 500 years old." He crawls out of the bush with the box in hand. Bill dances around him excitedly, saying, "Let's open it, let's open it! There could be gold in there, or diamonds. It looks like a treasure chest." But the box is built too strong for the boys to open. Robert says, "We'll go to my house. Dad has all kinds of tools in his workshop. We can cut the lock off the box."

Robert finds a hacksaw in his dad's workshop and cuts the lock off the box. The boys' eyes open wide as they pry the lid open. Much to their surprise, inside the box is another, smaller box. It is blue and looks to be solid. No hinges, no locks. It glows with white-blue energy. Without caution, Bill grabs the blue box and drops it quickly. "Ow, it burned me!" he exclaims, waving his hands to cool them. Robert says "Let me see." He very carefully touches the box with one fingertip. Frowning, he looks at Bill and picks the blue box up. "It feels cool and wet to me, not hot at all." The boys try every way possible to open the box. They use a hammer, a saw, even a blow torch, but they can not penetrate the blue box. Finally, they give up for the day. It is getting late. Robert takes the box up to his bedroom and sets it on the dresser by his bed. He is tired from all the excitement and falls asleep. About 2:00 a.m., the blue box begins to glow. A blue energy pours from the box lighting the bedroom with a soft glow. Robert turns in his sleep and his hand falls on top of the blue box. As he sleeps the blue energy is transmitted into his body. The veins in his hand glow blue with transferred energy. The energy moves up his arm until all the veins in his body light up like neon tubes filled with blue energy. An energy transfusion has taken place.

As daylight comes, the glow of the box disappears and Robert's body looks normal once again. He wakes up and looks at the box. He has a very strange feeling, as though he is united with whatever is in the blue box. He has a quick vision of outer space. In his vision a blue energy flash passes by a star. Robert shakes his head. "I must be losing my mind," he thinks. He puts the box in his dresser drawer for safe keeping. He has to go to school.

After school Robert hurries home and takes the box out of his dresser drawer. He holds the box for awhile, turning it over in his hands. As he looks at the box he becomes tired and falls asleep. His dreams again are of himself traveling in space in the form of light energy. Robert is awakened by his mother calling him to supper. After eating supper he returns to his bedroom and does his homework. He puts the box on the bed beside him and goes to sleep. About 2:00 a.m. the box begins to glow again, but this time much brighter. Robert's veins also glow with blue energy now. In his sleep, his hand reaches for the box. As his hand touches its cool surface, the box slowly opens.

Inside the box is a white-blue crystal. The crystal begins to emit a white energy that makes Robert's body levitate about two feet above the bed. The energy crystal levitates out of the box and positions itself about three feet above the floating boy. Then the crystal emits blue, green, red, then purple energies that bombard Robert's body. The blue energy in his veins changes to the colors that the crystal emits. Then the room goes black and Robert falls and hits the bed. When his body hits the bed, the scene changes and he sees himself on a mountaintop. The deep, powerful voice of the universe tells him of his mission on earth as Father Rock and as Father Rock, he will face the demon Demos in battle.

Robert awakened from the trance in a panic. "I am running out of time!" he thought.

FATHER ROCK

One

As he walked down the street, Robert heard a weather report coming from a car radio. It was a nice day, sunny, 81 degrees, a perfect day for the art festival downtown. A thief ran past him and stole a cup of money from a blind man sitting on the sidewalk. Across the street a priest helped an old lady carry her bags of food. Robert thought, "there are good and bad people in this world. It's too bad the world can't be full of people who do good things and help one another. Instead we see the hungry and homeless people, and all the criminals." He shook his head sadly. "C'est La Vie", he whispered, "Some things, we cannot change." Ahead, he saw a sign: ART SHOW TODAY.

Robert wound his way through the crowd to his display booth. His art work is representations of dimensional symbols, and there is a large collection on exhibition. He noticed a sixtyish man wearing an Irish beret holding a cane with a snake's head carved as a handle peering intently at one of his paintings. A sunbeam caught the faceted gems embedded in the cane's snake eyes and reflected green sparkles around him. Robert said, "Pardon me, sir, you seem to be very interested in this piece."

"Yes," the man replied, "I am much more than interested. This symbol is a quantum math form. I would like to meet the artist."

"I painted these. My name is Robert. And you are?" The man smiled and said, "Everyone calls me Dr. C. I am an archaeologist, among other things, haha. Secret missions, you know, all very hush-hush." He winked conspiratorially.

"Are you the famous Dr. C? The genius that discovered and deciphered the ancient writings from the islands?" "Guilty as charged! Yes, sir, I am he," Dr. C chuckled. His face flushed modestly, as if it surprised him to be recognized. "You know of my work?" "Oh, yes, sir, your papers are fascinating." Robert nodded. "It's my honor to meet you. You're very well known throughout the world." "Thank you!" Dr. C beamed and gestured at the paintings. "Now, about these symbols, do you know their meaning?"

Robert didn't answer the question but asked instead, "Would you care to work together on deciphering the math language?" Dr. C nodded enthusiastically. He enjoyed nothing more than a good puzzle, and deciphering this mysterious language looked like quite a challenge. He had a feeling that Robert would prove to be an interesting friend indeed.

Robert knew Dr. C would be a great help on the mission. Deciphering the math symbols would be a huge step forward and who better to work on it than a world-renown scholar? What a stroke of luck to meet him!

Dr. C said, "I have a colleague I would like to introduce you to. He is an aerospace engineer named Zoron. The quantum design art and symbols would fascinate him. How about setting a lunch date for tomorrow?" The men exchanged phone numbers.

FATHER ROCK

That evening Dr. C called to confirm lunch with Zoron for the next day. Robert felt good about his meeting with Dr. C and welcomed the possibility of Zoron working on the project. The expertise of an aerospace engineer would be invaluable. Before ending the call, Dr. C reminded Robert, “Be sure to bring samples of the symbols and the drawings to the lunch.” Robert answered, “Okay, I’ll see you tomorrow at one at the museum café.”

Promptly at one the next day, Robert entered the café and looked around. Immediately, he heard a loud voice with a strong Irish brogue calling. “Hello, hello! Over here!” Robert spotted Dr. C waving his cane in the air, anxiously signaling. “Over here.” He had a jolly personality. A man, presumably Zoron, stood beside Dr. C and just grinned. He was a striking man, tall, with black hair and green eyes. He was much younger than Robert expected him to be, maybe 28 or 29 years of age at most. *I think Zoron gets a kick out of Dr. C’s loud, open mannerisms*, thought Robert.

Two

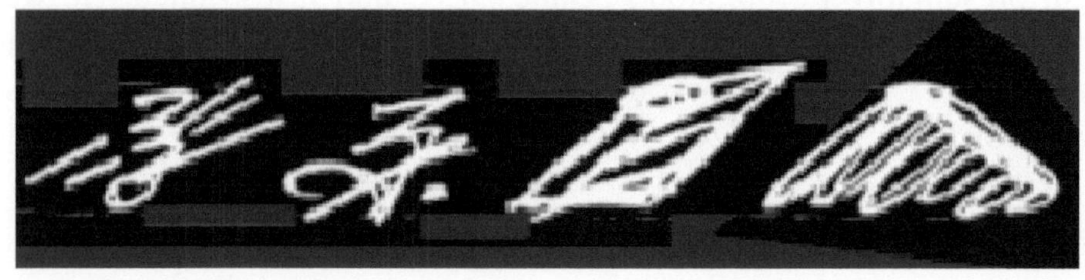

Robert had his art samples tucked under his arm in a black leather case. Zoron said anxiously, “So this is it? Let me see it.” Dr. C's eyebrows lifted. “Zoron, you haven’t even been properly introduced yet.” “Of course, where are my manners? Hello, Robert.” Zoron smiled sheepishly and shook hands with Robert. “I am just anxious to see what Dr. C has seen, the ‘magic language’, he called it. The quantum math symbols. Can I see them?” As Robert opened his leather case the air was filled with excitement. Zoron’s eyes popped open wide. At first glance, his mind raced. He turned page after page of math symbols, growing more excited with each symbol. Robert’s gaze was locked on Zoron’s face, reading his expressions. He hoped that Zoron could understand the message. After a few minutes of intense concentration, Zoron said, “This is the most advanced form of math I have ever seen. It's a math language of unearthly dimensions and the structural drawings are unlike anything I have ever heard of."

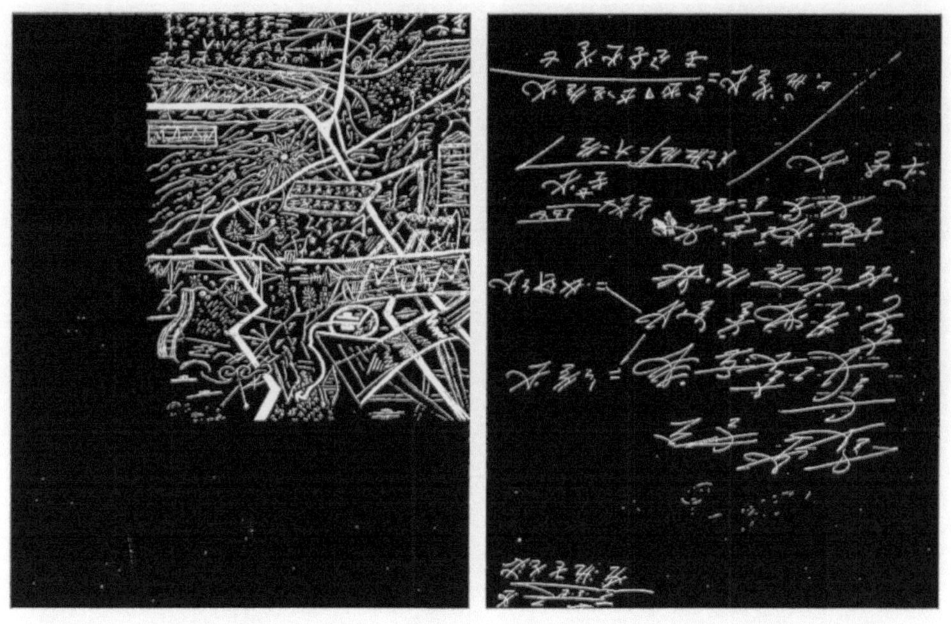

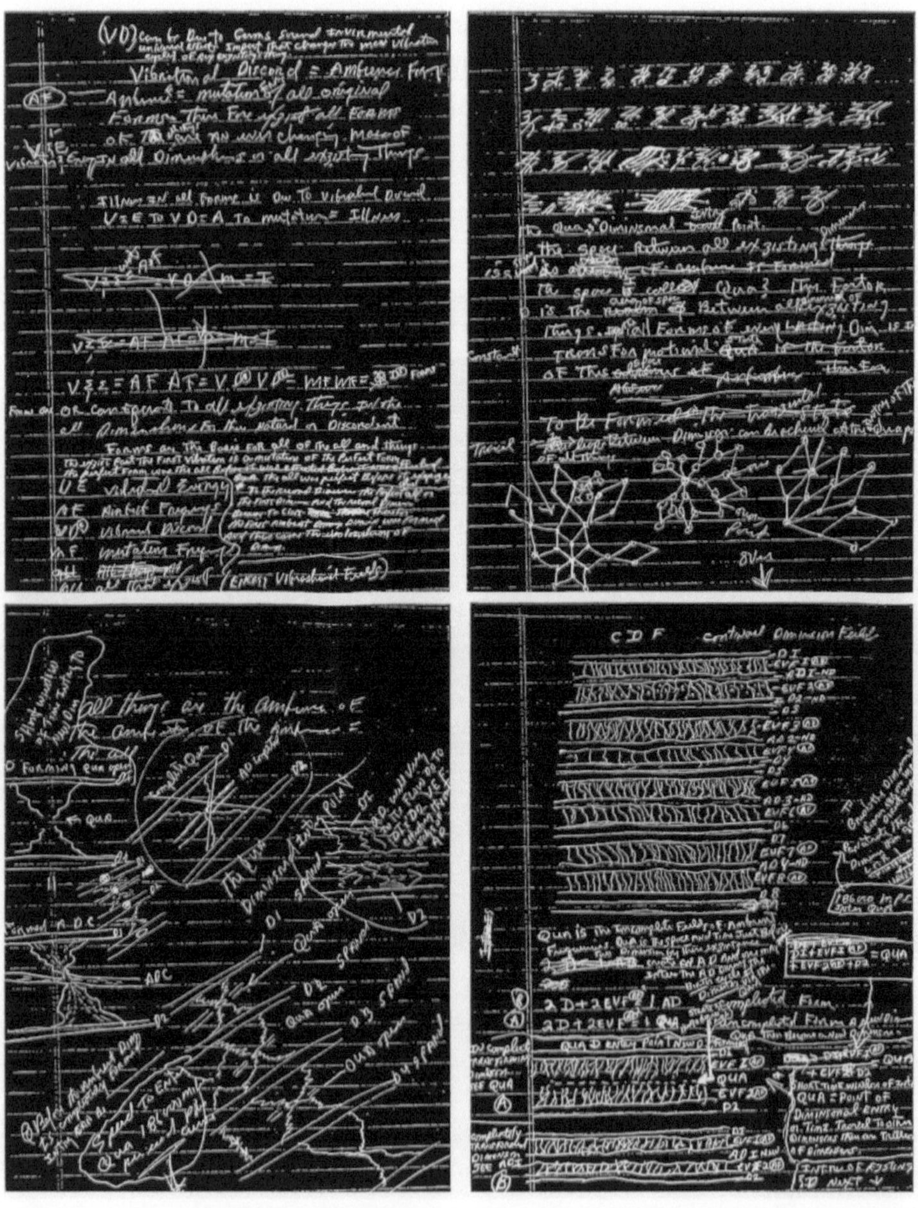

FATHER ROCK

TERRY BROOKS

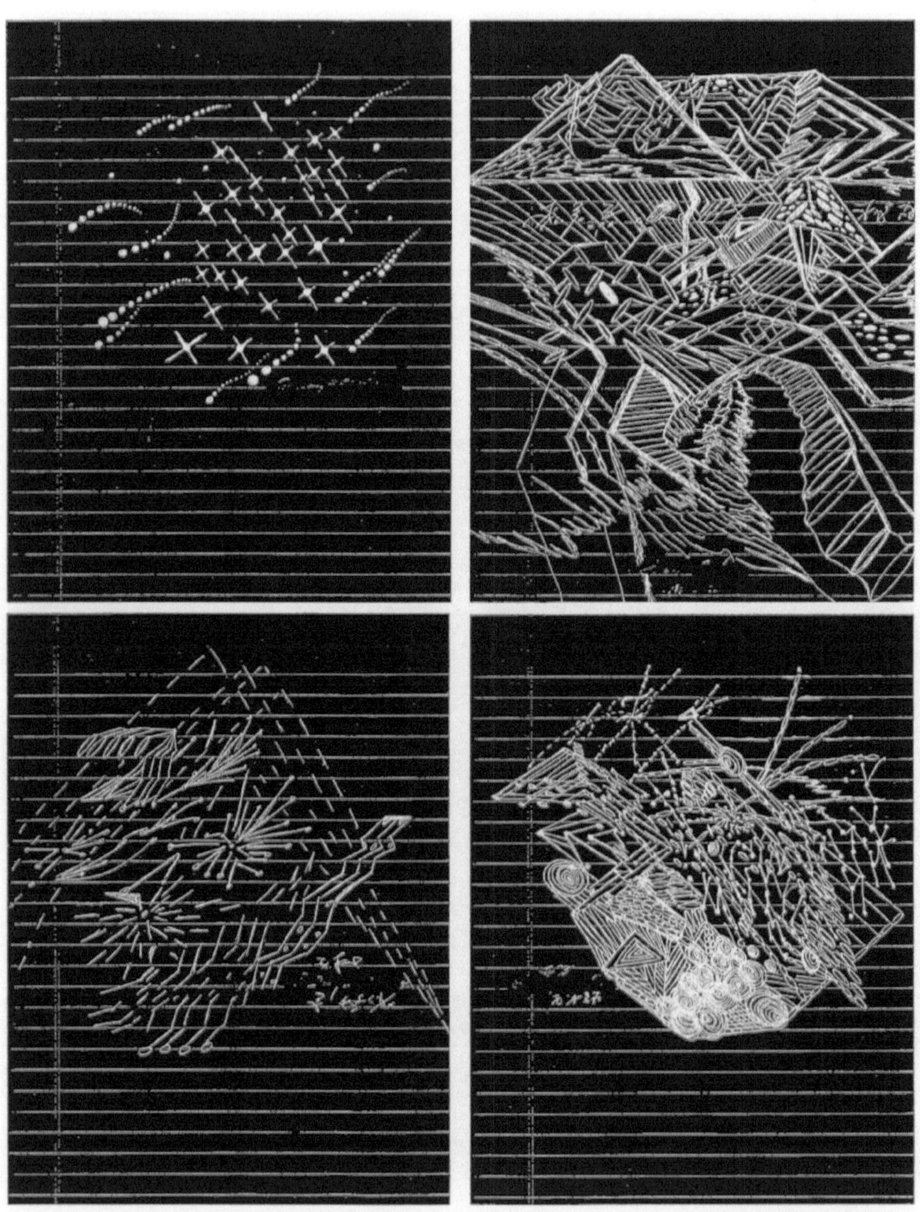

FATHER ROCK

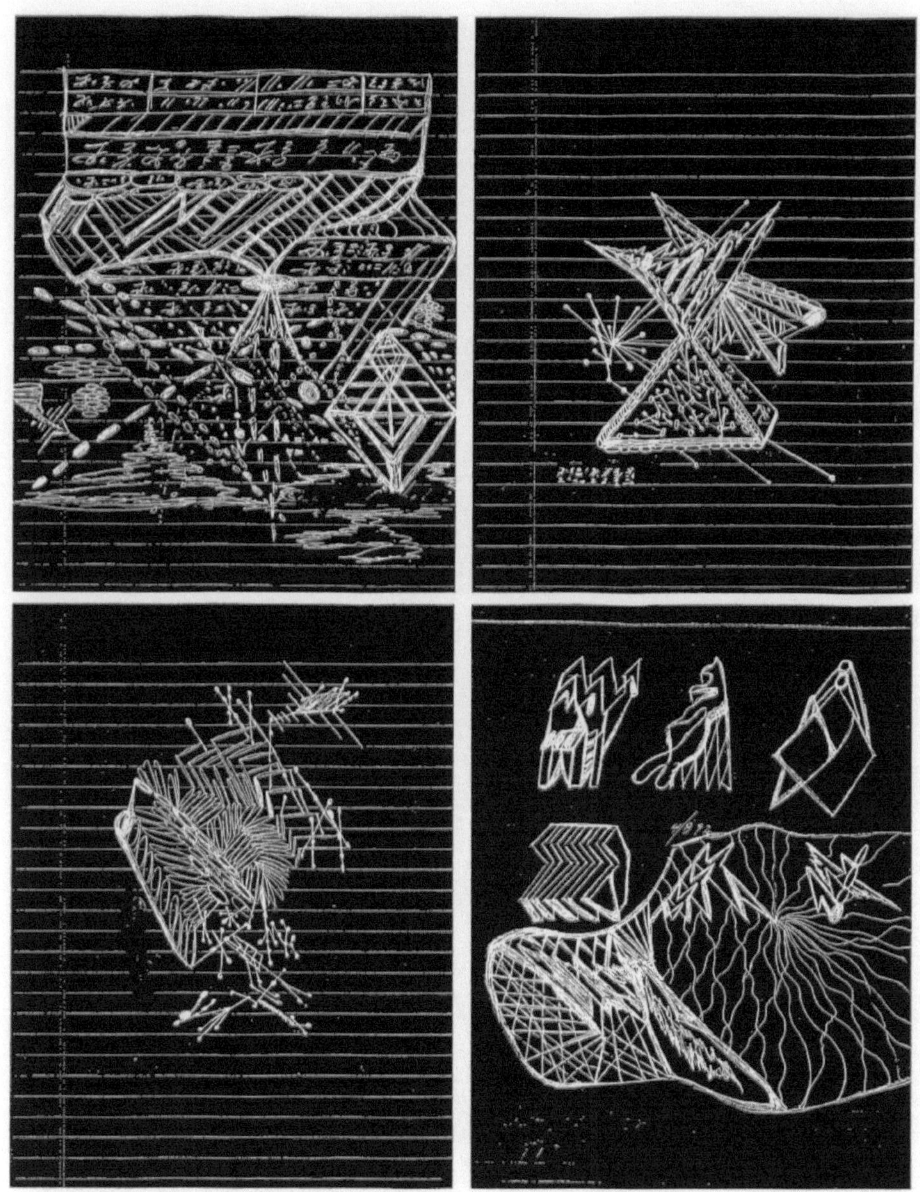

TERRY BROOKS

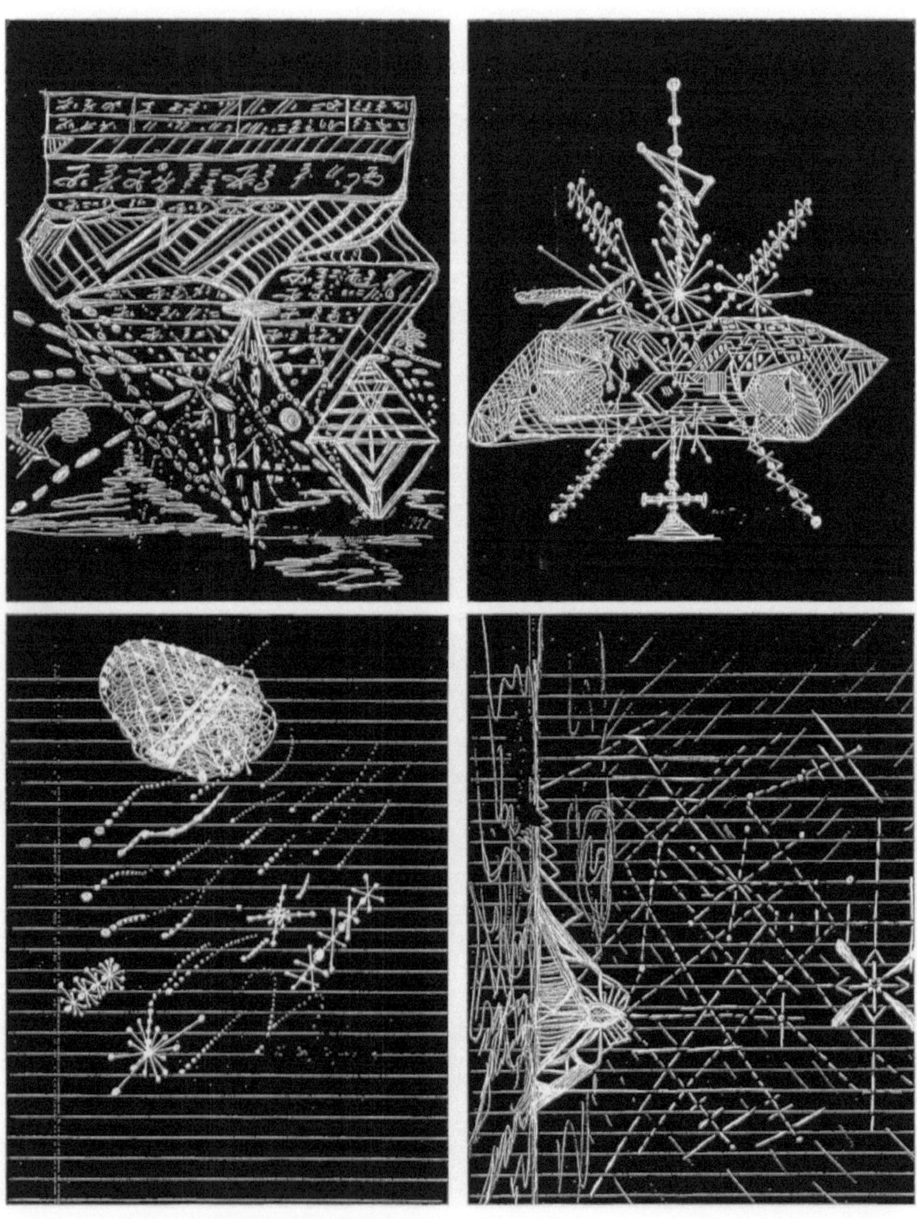

FATHER ROCK

TERRY BROOKS

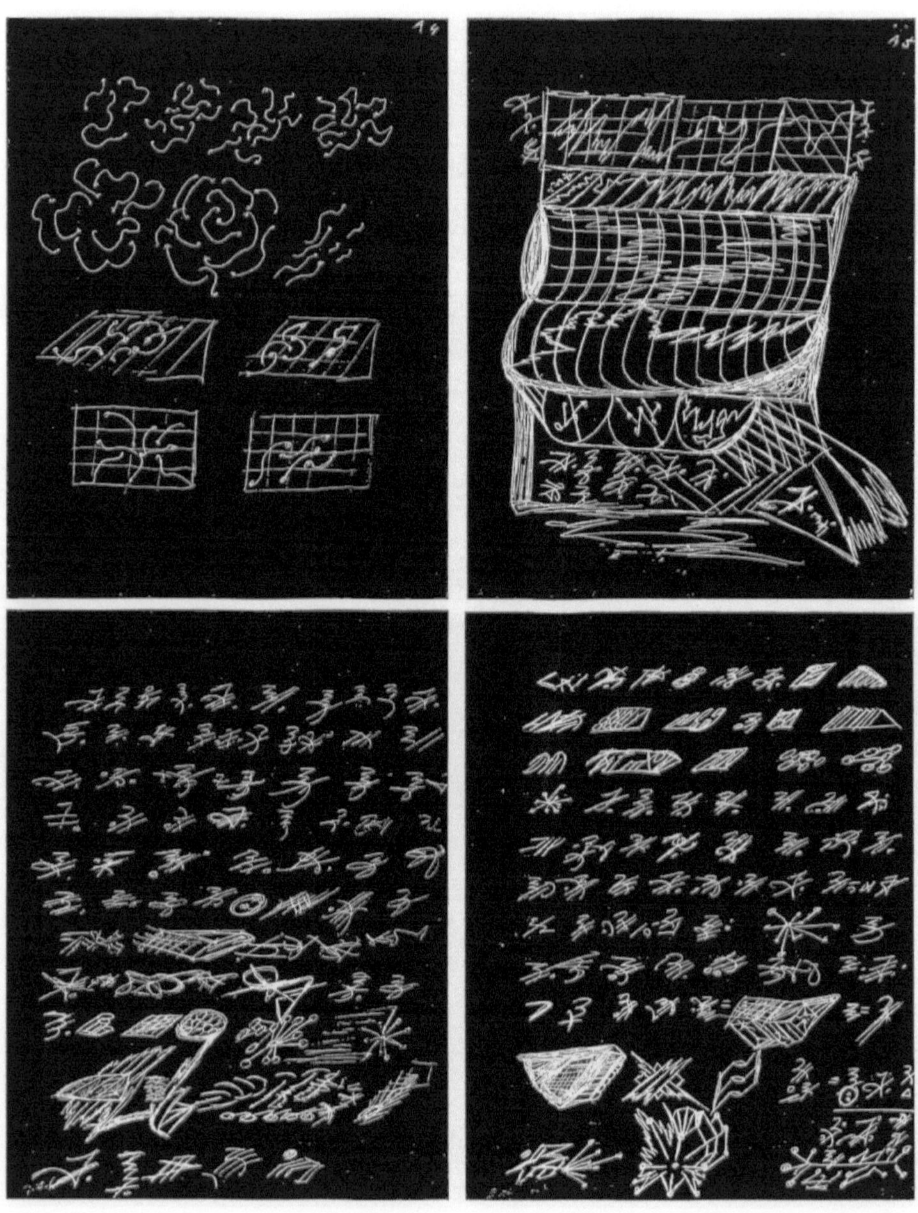

FATHER ROCK

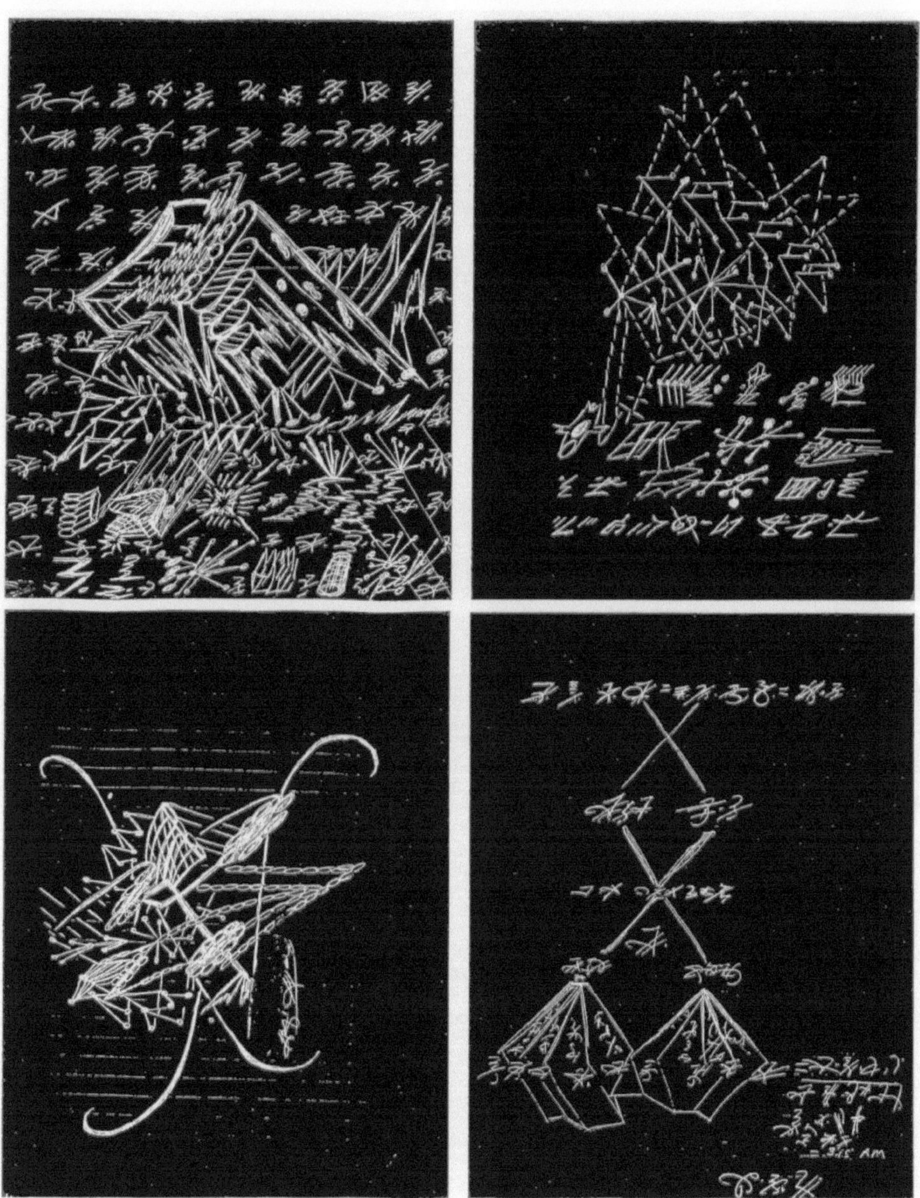

TERRY BROOKS

FATHER ROCK

Suddenly the room faded as Robert experienced a flashback. *Where the table was a moment ago, he sees a white energy burst zooming through space. Then a second energy burst zooming through space, a dark energy. As Robert sees a structural design pattern take shape, big beads of sweat form on his forehead. He senses a larger energy source and hears a voice saying, "As Father Rock, you will represent all good and positive forces in the Universe." A cult appears now. The cult members are gathered around a sacrificial table. They are wearing black satanic robes with hoods that cover their heads. They are reciting chants to summon a dark power.*

This power will become Demos. Demos will face Father Rock in battle on planet Earth.

Zoron asked, "What's wrong with Robert? Is he all right?"

Dr. C shook his head and put a finger to his lips. "He's in a trance. Don't say a word."

White energy races toward Earth. Vivid purple energy is also accelerating toward Earth; positive and negative forces shooting through space towards a single destination. Now he sees an ambulance racing down the highway. A pregnant woman is inside the ambulance. Robert hears the sound of a heartbeat pounding very loud and sees medics scurrying around the woman. She is getting ready to have a child. All at once the ambulance driver slams on the brakes and the ambulance skids sideways into an embankment. The woman falls to the floor, writhing in pain. They are trapped in the vehicle. Moving quickly, they lift the woman back onto the stretcher and call a rescue unit and medivac chopper to get them out.

Meanwhile at the cave the cult leaders are chanting "Demos, Demos." They are bringing forth another woman who is pregnant from a dark corridor. They carry blazing torches. They lay the woman's grand body on a table. She will soon have the child who will become Demos.

Robert awakened from the trance but did not remember what had just happened. He remembered only bits and pieces of the vision.

Dr. C asked, “Robert, are you okay?” Robert took a napkin from the table and wiped his forehead. “I’m okay, I’m okay,” he said, taking a drink of water.

Zoron asked, “What happened?” Robert decided he might as well tell them to see how they would react. “I had a vision of myself traveling in space in the form of energy.” Dr. C and Zoron looked at each other and nodded. “I think we have heard enough.” Zoron took Dr. C's arm and they hurried towards the door.

Three

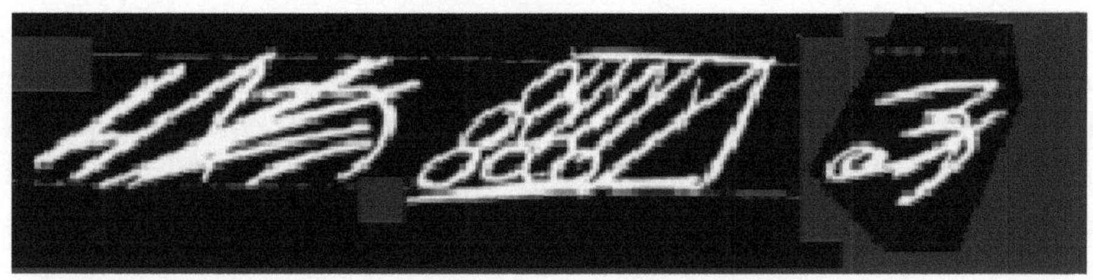

Disoriented, Robert closed his eyes, thinking perhaps they left because they did not understand the message, or because they thought him insane. The vision continued.

The chopper has now picked up the first woman and moved her to the hospital. As they are unloading the woman at the hospital, Robert sees a positive energy force racing through outer space toward the planet Earth.

The vision moves back to the cave where the mysterious cult has now laid the pregnant woman's body on a sacrificial table. A loud, eerie sound of purple energy is racing, accelerating, and approaching the woman on the sacrificial table. At the hospital, the doctor works very quickly to help the pregnant woman. The two women are simultaneously having children. The positive energy force is racing very fast. It knocks open the door to the hospital. As the positive energy force goes through the door, the energy moves in slow motion. The blue-white energy force is seeking the child at the hospital. The energy force moves quickly to the operating room then the energy knocks open the operating room doors. All the people around the table go into a trance. They will have no memory of this energy entering the room. The baby at this time is in the doctor's arms. As the energy goes into the baby's third eye, a very high, shrill guitar note sounds; the baby trembles and vibrates. It lights up with the blue energy as all of the energy races through the baby's third eye. Father Rock is born.

In the cave the cult is chanting "Demos, Demos" and as a cult member holds this child in the air the negative forces enter through that child's third eye and baby "Demos'" skin turns red, then purple. His eyes are black; his face turns bright green then pink. A dark purple energy beam shoots out of baby Demos' mouth and a very powerful low sound is heard. The cult chants, "Demos, Demos, Demos is born."

Four

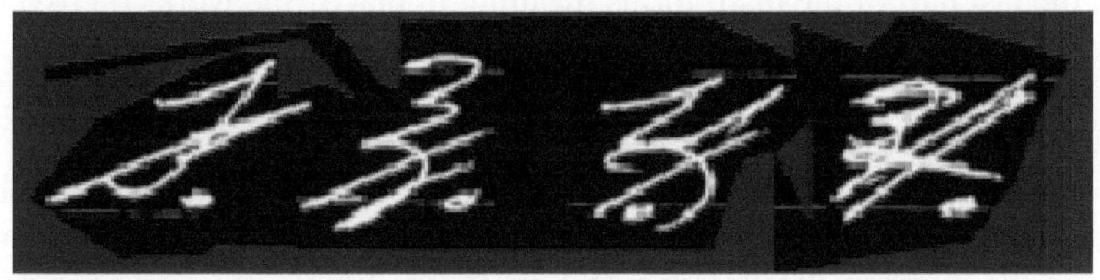

Robert felt a hand on his shoulder; it was Zoron. He and Dr. C had come back. He said, “We have discussed it, and we would like to study the symbols more, to try and decipher them. Will you trust us with this?” Robert sighed, relieved that the two scientists wanted to decipher the message. If anyone could break the mathematical code, they were the ones. Robert answered, “Yes, of course.” Zoron took the leather case and left with Dr. C, talking rapidly as they walked away. Robert put his hand inside his shirt and rubbed his unicrystal necklace. "What will I do if they don’t understand it?" he wondered.

A week passed with no word from Dr. C or Zoron. Then Robert got a morning phone call. “This is Dr. C, Robert,” said the anxious voice, “we must see you right away. We have information about the symbols. Can we meet at the same place at noon?” Dr. C agreed. “Fine, I’ll see you then. I'll bring Zoron."

The museum café was not crowded and Zoron was easy to spot, since he was waving his arms in the air, talking excitedly. He didn't even pause for a hello before launching into conversation. "Dr. C and I have some interpretations of the math language. It has something to do with time travel or space travel. We believe that the energy you see while you are in a trance is coming to earth." Robert nodded thinking, *They are on the right track, but they are far from getting the message. We must work faster.*

Zoron continued, "Dr. C and I want to consult another colleague of ours, Jean Lang, who is a psychic as well as a physicist. She probably can put the last part of the math forms meaning in place. She works on psychic phenomenon projects all over the world."

Robert said, "Sounds like she'll be a great addition to the team. Can you call her today?"

Zoron nodded. "She is at the university in the physics and psychic research center. I can call her right now." He pulled out his cell phone and dialed the number. "Hello Jean, this is Zoron. I have run into something that I am sure will interest you. I have met this guy named Robert. Dr. C called me in to see the quantum math and dimensional art this man creates. After a week of study Dr. C and I managed to break some of the math language code of symbols. I think your knowledge and psychic intuitiveness is needed. Can you meet with us to examine these documents?" Jean replied coolly, but inside she was excited. "Of course, it sounds very interesting. I'm up for a new project. Come over to my house around 7:00 p.m. Bring Dr. C and Robert with you and we shall begin by looking at the symbols in my study."

Jean prepared her study to run some tests on Robert. He would not be aware of these tests. These tests would determine whether or not he was receiving some intuitive forces of extraterrestrial influence. Jean placed a thin piece of red crystal on a table. Jean wanted to hear Robert's comments about the crystal. She put a blue piece of crystal in a bowl. She wanted to see if Robert picked up the blue or red crystal or if he just ignored the crystals totally. If Robert were drawn to the blue crystal this would mean a lot to Jean's evaluation of his karmic energy levels. She placed two magnets on the table not touching. She wanted to see if he would place the magnets together to connect the magnetic energy fields.

At the same time she could do a psychic reading on Robert's aura. She was ready for an interesting evening. At 7:00 p.m. the doorbell rang. "Right on time," said Jean. Standing by the door was Zoron. "Hi Jean," he said and introduced everyone. "You know Dr. C and this is Robert." Jean could not believe her eyes. Robert had a blue white aura of energy around him. She stared at him as if looking through an energy haze. Apparently Dr. C and Zoron could not see this energy field around their new friend. When Robert looked into her eyes, he knew she could see his karmic field. Robert said, "Jean, it's been a few thousand years since I last saw you." Jean eyes were glazed. She went into a trance and envisioned herself in a white robe. She was spinning and dancing to strange music. An old man was playing his music with a light of some kind. "Oh," Jean said, "Yes, hello Robert." Dr. C and Zoron thought Robert was joking when he said, I haven't seen you for a thousand years, but Jean knew they had a connection, something old and mysterious and deep. This was his way of saying to her; I am back, do you remember?

They were connecting on a cosmic level. Picking up on Robert's thoughts, Jean saw energy, white-hot energy flying through space. Symbols, dimensional designs, a lot of different colored energies, all flew in different directions at once. Robert put his hand in Jean's hand and shock waves of energy hit in her mind's eye. No one else could see the inner storm. She was the only one who could read Robert's energy. Jean took a deep breath and said, "Let's sit down and take a look at the symbols." When the leather case was opened Jean put her hand on top of the stack of symbols and closed her eyes. She felt tremendous waves of energy and she passed out.

Robert wet a cloth and touched it to Jean's face. She awakened and said, “I remember you, you are the one to face Demos.” Dr. C and Zoron erupted with anxious questions, “Who is Demos?" "What is going on here, Jean?" “You remember Robert?” "How and when did you know him, and what does this “Demos” have to do with it?” Jean put her hands up to slow the barrage of questions and shook her head. “Robert was sent to Earth to face evil forces in a battle in the future; that’s all I can tell you now.”

Dr. C looked puzzled, “But we need to know more, if we are to be part of the team.” Zoron nodded in agreement. Jean said, “We are supposed to help Robert. I will tell you when I can.” Dr. C said, “Okay, fine. I trust your judgment. How can we help?” “Zoron,” Jean said, “you must build an energy machine to transport Robert’s helpers. The blueprints are here but in dimensional math. I will help decipher the symbols so you can build the time dimensional device to bring the rest of the formulas needed to prepare the team.” Zoron said, “Team? What team?” Jean said, “The team is scattered throughout the world. When they see the symbols they will remember the mission on this planet.” “There is a mission? Jean, what mission? We’re lost. We don’t know what you’re talking about. Explain more to us.” Zoron's brow furrowed. “The mission…you don’t understand, we must get ready for the mission. Robert shall become Father Rock and must face Demos in battle. There’s a mission to unite good people around the world to fight all evil. As the members contact us we shall form an organization called ‘Team United Worldwide', or 'TUW’. TUW will help Father Rock face Demos in battle. I’ll tell you more later. But for now let's get to work on the time transporter. Once we have the time transporter built, you will understand everything in detail.” Dr. C and Zoron said, “Jean, with all due respect, we are completely lost and do not know of what you’re trying to achieve. You’re talking like a crazy person. Demos, who is Demos? The energy forces, the structural designs, dimensional quantum; what is all this?” Jean said, “Everything will become clear in the near future. You must trust me and assist Robert. That’s all I can say at this time.”

Five

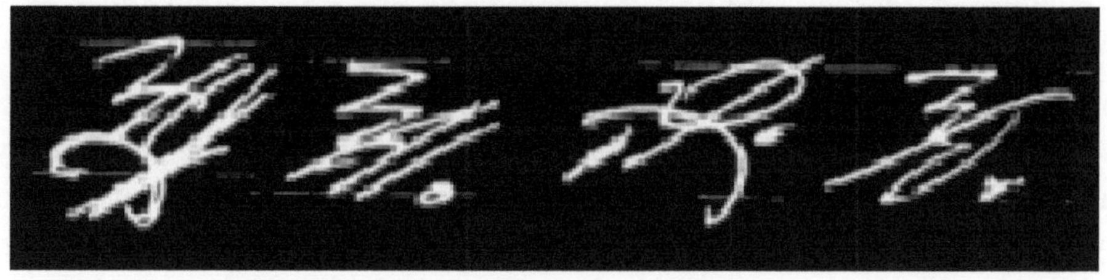

Jean said, "Time is short, we must get started. Give me the stack of dimensional art forms and let's build this thing. Okay?" Zoron said, "Let's do it."

Jean and Zoron took all of the papers and spread them on Jean's study room floor. Robert and Dr. C were out on the patio going over some quantum math expressions. Robert knew he had now found the first three members of the team: Dr. C, Zoron, and Jean.

Jean and Zoron worked fast. One of the pieces of equipment needed was a super powerful booster. The only thing that fit the bill was a new power source, the XX49. There were only two in the world, one located at NASA and one in Russia. Zoron said, "Jean, without the XX49 power booster we cannot build the time transporter. Robert's blueprint designs show we can't get enough power unless we have the XX49. Do you know who is in charge of the XX49? Nerdboy Baxter." Jean said, "Oh, no, not Nerdboy." Zoron said, "Yep. You know, Jean, Baxter has always had a crush on you." He winked at her playfully. Jean put her hand up in protest, "Oh no! Oh no! I'm not going to play up to him to get the XX49."

"You guys, I hate you," Jean said as they rode in Zoron's car the next day to the lab at NASA. "You owe me big time." They pulled up to the security gate. Zoron showed his ID to the guard, "We are here to see Nerdboy. I mean Dr. Neville Baxter." Jean slapped Zoron on the shoulder and said again, "You owe me, buddy." They pulled up to the building and went into Nerd's lab. There he was, Nerdboy, just as Jean remembered him. He hadn't slept in two days; his hair stuck up at odd angles, and thick horn-rimmed glasses, slipped down a very big nose. He hadn't moved from his computer for 10 hours while talking to himself and scratching his head.

Nerd's IQ was off the charts. His tee shirt read, "I am smart and you know it." Zoron said, "Baxter, Baxter!" Baxter spun around in his chair, saying, "Ugh, oh, ah, hi," brushing his wiry hair with his hands. Nerd's white lab coat had tomato splashes all over it from pizza and mustard stains. Nerd said, "Jean, you look great." Jean ran a hand through her long chestnut hair and widened her blue eyes, turning her considerable charms on the hapless scientist, "Thank you, Baxter." she smiled sweetly. Flustered, Baxter knocked a cup of coffee all over the table. "Come over here and sit down," Baxter said. "I have coffee and doughnuts. Gee, no one comes to see me." "We've heard you invented an XX49 power booster, the most powerful booster in the world. It sounds so exciting." Jean leaned forward and put a manicured hand on his arm. "True. True." Nerdboy beamed proudly. Nerdboy was known for his gigantic ego. "True, but it's top secret." "Can we see it?" Jean played her role to the hilt, batting her eyes like a schoolgirl. "Well, I don't know," said Baxter. Jean squeezed his arm, "If I were you I would be so proud of that type of accomplishment." Nerdboy's chest swelled with pride and he said, "Well okay, I have it in my safe. As long as you don't tell anyone." As Nerdboy opened the safe he looked back over his shoulder to be sure no one could see the safe combination.

Nerdboy took out a small chrome box and popped the lid up. “Here it is.” It was a round, black, shiny, metallic-looking object. “Wow!” they said. “That’s great, Baxter.” Zoron looked on the table where there was a pizza with a round, black olive the same size as the XX49 power booster. Zoron pulled Jean aside and said, “Do you think you can get Baxter away from the box for a couple of seconds?” “I’ll try,” She walked up to Baxter and stood real close to him, looking at the XX49. Then Jean touched his hand and he looked longingly at her. She fluttered her eyelashes at him, the way she imagined a love-struck teenager would.

Baxter was overwhelmed by this attention from Jean. As Baxter looked into her eyes and tried to stammer something interesting, Zoron palmed the XX49 out of the chrome box and put the black olive in its place. Jean could not believe her eyes. "We are all going to jail", she thought. Jean reached out and closed the box lid, without taking her eyes off Baxter's. She said, “Thanks Baxter, your XX49 is brilliant.” Nerdboy said, “Yeah, but remember, you promised you won't tell anyone. I should have not shown you the XX49. It is top secret and it cost fifteen million dollars to develop.” Baxter cradled the chrome box in his arms as if it were his baby and put the box back into the safe, spinning the combination and looking back with a grin. Nerdboy said, “The XX49 is to be used next week as the main power booster on a half-billion-dollar rocket launch. I need not tell you all if it’s found out that you’ve seen the XX49, we’ll all be in trouble.” Everyone said good-bye and the team left. Jean was steaming at Zoron. “Are you mad? We all could go to jail for life.” Jean continued saying, “Stealing government property, and disclosure of a top secret; national security breach. You’re all nuts! You are all nuts!” Zoron patted her hand reassuringly. “We only need the XX49 for two days. We'll have it back before he even notices it missing." Jean did not feel reassured. "Two days and that’s it! We’re putting it back whether we’re finished with it or not. Have you even considered how?” “Baxter may have a hopeless crush, but he's not stupid. He will know something is up when we show up at the lab again." "Maybe", Zoron answered, "but you heard him. If anyone finds out he showed us the XX49, Nerdboy will be in as much trouble as we will. So it's in his best interest to take it back quietly." "I don't like it, but I guess it's the only plan we have", Jean grumbled. Her eyes were troubled, but she lapsed into silence.

They went back to Jean's house to work all night. By morning, the first stage of the time transporter was built. Zoron said, "All we have to do is place the XX49 in the charge chamber for two days." They all watched as Zoron put the XX49 in the machine. Click. It snapped in place. Two small arms clamped down on the small power booster. "A flashing light," Zoron said, "see, it's working. In two days we'll take the XX49 back to Nerdboy and NASA won't ever know it was taken. Everything will be fine. Let the time transporter charge and we'll go home and get some sleep. Everyone is tired."

None of the team really felt good about stealing Baxter's XX49. But the team understood if they didn't take the XX49 there would be no world to worry about. The team's mission was so important that this had to be done to save everyone and all existing things. The next morning Jean awoke to find the light blinking faster. The time transporter was being energized. The day passed by slowly for the team. They waited in great anticipation to see what would happen after the first part of the time transporter, the brain, was charged.

The two days passed and Jean called the team to her home. The light on the machine now glowed steadily. The charging phase was completed. The XX49 had done the job. The team huddled around. Zoron said, "Here goes." He flipped a switch and the XX49 extended out of the time transporter on a small arm. Then a small button was exposed behind a sliding door. Zoron put the XX49 carefully into a small box and put the box in his pocket. "We'll get this back to the Nerd today." Jean nodded. "I'll feel much better about this once we've returned it." A low hum came from the time transporter. Zoron pushed a button, and a section of the wall turned into a viewing screen, eight feet by eight feet in size.

Symbols flashed across the screen. A vivid blue flash of energy came out of the screen and enveloped Robert, pulling him into the picture onscreen. The team watched as Robert's image appeared on the screen, standing on a mountaintop. Light played around him as Robert's image changed. Moments later, Robert, was transported back to the front room. Dr. C, Jean and Zoron couldn't believe their eyes. Bright colors set a rhythmic pattern around him and he had completely changed. "Father Rock," was a white-haired wizard with a long white beard wearing a robe. He was a highly spiritual looking entity, a time traveler from another dimension with a laser guitar in his hand. The time transporter was loading information from another dimension dating back to the beginning of time. The team watched in amazement, trying to comprehend the information bombarding them. They were struggling to understand that Robert was "Father Rock," sent to earth to fight the evil Demos, and, that they were to help him in the battle.

Twenty-four hours later the time transporter was still downloading information. Zoron said, "Let's call it a night." Everyone went home. First thing the next day Jean ran into her study to see the time transporter. It was flashing, downloading, then all at once letters formed. Jean knocked a vase off of a table while grabbing the phone, she was so excited. She conference-called the team and said, "The big screen is ready. In large green letters it says, "TRANSMISSION COMPLETED."

Six

Jean was so excited that she didn't want to be bothered, but she had to check her e-mail for work messages. She turned on her computer. A voice said, "You have mail." Jean said, "What 18,156 e-mails! That's impossible. What is this?" Jean opened her first e-mail. It said, "I was watching the world news and a shot of art work with a symbol caught my attention. The work was by Robert. I feel I must know more about this symbol. I am on standby, I am on standby." There was e-mail after e-mail from all over the world. People were drawn to the symbol in the art. Each one said at the closing of their e-mail, "I am on standby, I am on standby." The symbol had triggered subconscious knowledge that they were part of the team.

More e-mails, Jean flashed through more from England, Germany, Italy, China, Japan, India, Africa, all over the world and the USA. Father Rock, Dr. C and Zoron arrived and looked at the e-mails. Father Rock nodded in satisfaction. “Meet Team United Worldwide. Looks like things are falling into place.” He looked around at the scientists gathered in the room. "We will be known as the Team Leaders."

The Team Leaders sat before the time transporter in a kind of daze. What next? The past two weeks had been bizarre. Everyone’s life had been turned upside down, Dr. C’s, Zoron’s, and Jean’s. All their jobs were in jeopardy. None of them were going to their day jobs. It all seemed so overwhelming. Dr. C said, “Well I guess I should push this button. Once we do that, there's no turning back..” Everyone just sighed. “Hhhhh.” None of them was ready for any more. “Okay, let’s take a vote. Thumbs-up for yes.” Jean, she slowly gave the thumbs-up. Dr. C, “Oh well, what the heck.” He gave the thumbs-up. Zoron said, “I guess it’s up to me. Okay, it’s unanimous, let's do it.” Zoron reached for the red button. He heard knocking and yelling at the front door. “Olives! I’ve got olives!” “Uh, oh, it’s Nerdboy! He’s found the olive. I forgot to return the XX49.” Zoron opened the door. Baxter’s eyes were crazy with anger. “Where’s my XX49? You stole it. We will all lose our jobs, even worse; we will all go to jail. We’ll be disgraced in the scientific community. Oh no, oh, no.” Zoron tried to calm him saying, “Baxter, Baxter, wait. We have your XX49 right here. Look, look, here it is.” “Let me see,” Baxter said, “let me see.” His eyes lit up as Zoron opened his hand. “Here it is. It’s not hurt. It’s fine.” Baxter snatched it, “Give me that! No one can ever know this happened.” He stomped to the door. Throwing his arms into the air, he turned around and threw the olive at Zoron. Baxter screamed, “My lab is off limits to all of you, OFF limits!” He mumbled as he walked down the hall. “Off limits, I never want to see any of you again.” Zoron closed the door. They were all shaken by Baxter’s ranting and raving. They looked at one another. “This is a mess. We committed a federal offense.” Dr. C shook his head. “I can't do this. I want out.” “No, you’re in. You know too much and you’re in,” Father Rock crossed his arms and faced them. "You know how important this is. No matter what goes wrong, we cannot back down." He knew time was running out. Demos would be coming soon with the demons. "He's right," said Jean, "We have to push the red button." “I’ll do it,” said Zoron. Before anyone could object, Zoron reached out and pushed the red button. The screen on the wall started to show pin-like dots: red, green, yellow, blue, brown and bright white dots. They all shimmered and changed colors. “It’s some kind of code,” said Dr. C. “But this does not help us. We can’t understand this. After we built this piece of equipment we were supposed to understand the mission, find out who Demos is and understand how we are to help Father Rock. And, by the way, where did Father Rock come from?”

The color patterns just kept coming and coming. A word formed in the pattern. “NOW” then another word “IS” then “THE TIME.” “NOW IS THE TIME.” The next line of words came, “FOR YOU TO UNDERSTAND THE MESSAGE, TO UNDERSTAND ALL THERE IS AND ALL THERE IS TO COME, TO PREPARE FATHER ROCK TO FACE DEMOS.”

The deep voice boomed from the wall. “FATHER ROCK FACED DEMOS IN ANOTHER DIMENSION BEFORE AND LOST.” The team looked at Father Rock. The voice said “FATHER ROCK IS IN A TRANCE AND CAN SEE AND HEAR ONLY THOSE PARTS OF THIS TRANSMISSION THAT I DEEM NECESSARY. HIS MEMORY OF FACING DEMOS BEFORE HAS BEEN ERASED. THIS WAY HE WILL HAVE NO FEAR."

The large screen was filled with quarter-size dots flashing in multiple colors. The deep heavy voice spoke again. “FATHER ROCK, THE MUZOIDS CREATED TWO SUPER ROBOTS. THEY ARE NAMED GOODTOR ROBOTS. DEMOS HAS STOLEN ONE OF THE GOODTOR ROBOTS AND PROGRAMMED IT TO DO HIS EVIL DEEDS.”

Father Rock said, “Oh no.” The team looked on, as the voice continued. “SO YOU NOW HAVE THREE LEVELS OF BATTLE. ONE – THE ROBOTS WILL BATTLE, GOODTOR ROBOT AND EVIL ROBOT. TWO – TUW, LED BY THE TEAM LEADERS, AND THE

MUZOIDS WILL FACE DEMOS' DEMONS, AND THREE – FATHER ROCK, YOU MUST FACE DEMOS IN BATTLE AND THIS BATTLE WILL BE THE DECIDING FACTOR OF WHETHER GOOD OR EVIL PREVAILS ON THE EARTH AND ALL EXISTING THINGS THROUGH INFINITE TIME. YOU MUST CONQUER DEMOS. HE HAS ALREADY PUT TOGETHER A LARGE CULT FOLLOWING TO ASSIST HIM IN BATTLE. SO I'LL MAKE THIS VERY BRIEF. IN THE BEGINNING A TRILLION BILLION LIGHT YEARS AGO TWO ENERGY FORCES WERE CREATED. ONE ENERGY FORCE OF GOOD THE OTHER ENERGY FORCE OF EVIL."

"THERE HAVE BEEN MANY BATTLES ON THIS TERRIBLE WAR BEFORE BETWEEN THE DARK AND THE LIGHT. FATHER ROCK IS THE LIGHT FORCE OF ALL GOOD THINGS THAT EXIST AND DEMOS REPRESENTS THE DARK POWERS OF ALL THINGS THAT EXIST."

"IN A BATTLE THAT TOOK PLACE ABOUT ONE MILLION OF YOUR YEARS AGO. IN THE DARK SECTOR OF THE THIRD SPECTOR DIMENSION, FATHER ROCK AND DEMOS BATTLED FOR 1000 OF YOUR EARTH YEARS. HUNDREDS OF MILLIONS OF LIFE FORMS WERE KILLED INCLUDING FATHER ROCK'S MOTHER AND FATHER. WHEN THIS BATTLE BEGAN, FATHER ROCK WAS A YOUNG BOY AND HIS FATHER WAS THE LIGHT. HIS FATHER WAS KILLED BEFORE FATHER ROCK WAS READY TO ASSUME THE LIGHT."

"NOW YOU ALL UNDERSTAND THE REASON THAT I PUT FATHER ROCK IN A TRANCE. THE PAIN OF THE LOSS OF HIS PARENTS IS TOO GREAT FOR HIM TO BEAR. ALTHOUGH FATHER ROCK IS THE STRONG AND POWERFUL LEADER OF ALL POSITIVE ENERGY, THE LOSS OF HIS MOTHER AND FATHER GAVE DEMOS THE ADVANTAGE, AND DEMOS WOUNDED FATHER ROCK IN THE NEXT BATTLE. WITH THAT DEFEAT, AN ENTIRE DIMENSION WAS LOST TO THE

DARKNESS. FATHER ROCK HAS NOW RECUPERATED AND GROWN STRONGER. HE IS READY TO REJOIN THE BATTLE."

The voice continued, "THIS IS THE FINAL BATTLE, FOR THIS DIMENSION SERVES AS THE GATEWAY TO THE LIGHT."

The viewer fell silent for a few moments to allow the team to digest this information. They were beginning to grasp the nature of the conflict.

"I WILL NOW TELL YOU ABOUT FATHER ROCK AND DEMOS. TWO ENERGY CHARGES WERE SENT FORWARD TO DO BATTLE ON EARTH. AT BIRTH, ROBERT, RECEIVED THE POSITIVE ENERGY FORCE OF FATHER ROCK AND DON, RECEIVED THE NEGATIVE DARK PURPLE ENERGY FORCE CALLED DEMOS. ROBERT WAS UNAWARE OF HIS MISSION ON THIS PLANET UNTIL THE AGE OF SEVENTEEN WHEN HE WAS ENLIGHTENED. AS A BOY, ROBERT HAD MANY POWERFUL GIFTS."

FATHER ROCK

Seven

The viewer screen showed everything the voice was saying. The team saw the universal energies traveling to earth and the boys, Robert and Don, receiving the energy. The voice said to the team, "WATCH ROBERT AS A YOUNG BOY OF FIVE."

Robert was playing outside, when a streak of light and energy hit the ground. Robert saw the flash and walked over to where the flash had hit. There was a beautiful crystal; red, blue, and green colors were sparkling in the sun. Many different colors were flickering from the crystal. Robert picked the crystal up and felt its' energy. He smiled. An energy aura of blue-white energized his body. Then Robert opened his hand, and the crystal was gone. "NOW YOU SEE A DARK ENERGY IS FLYING THROUGH THE NIGHT. DEMOS IS COMING. IN THE FORM OF BLACK-PURPLE ENERGY, DEMOS HITS A LARGE STONE AND MELTS IT. THE MELTED STONE RAISES FROM THE GROUND

AND FORMS DEMOS."

"Ha, ha, Father Rock, I know you will be on the planet Earth in the future and I shall destroy you." Demos could change to any form. Demos says, "I must change into a young boy." So Demos waves his hand and becomes a five-year-old boy. Demos thinks, "My name can't be Demos. So I'll call myself, Don. That's it. Don. Ha Ha. I must find a family to hide with while I set my plan in action."

A family is walking through a park. They are dressed in Victorian style clothing. Don walks up. The nice couple looks at Don and says, "What a cute boy." He zaps the family with his evil energy. The family takes Demos, Don now, as their own child. They are under Demos' power.

Now the viewer is showing Robert at the age of nine. *Robert had his second experience of alien power. A snake was ready to strike Robert and he called upon the power of good to protect him. The snake was rendered harmless.*

Demos had the adopted family under a spell. Nine-year-old Demos was standing at the head of a sacrificial table in his robe and hooded garb. The room was full of people in robes and they were all chanting, "Demos, Demos, Demos." Demos was preparing his demons and cult to fight Robert in the future. He would grow to adulthood in this body, build his evil horde, and then depart to be reborn again with Robert, the light to his dark. His cult would carry on with preparations as he rested for the final battle.

The team next saw Robert at the age of 14 in the viewer. *Robert was playing ball and the ball bounced over the fence in the path of a car. Robert put his hands forward and sent a blue-white energy force field that stopped the car.*

Robert's mind again flashed back to his experience with the crystal and then the snake. Robert remembered the same feeling had come over him, this feeling of alien power from another time and dimension. Now Robert could not help but wonder, "How do I have this power and where did it come from?" The team saw all this through Robert's eyes, sharing his thoughts and his wonder.

Next they saw Don as a young adult. Don was saying, "*Father Rock, Father Rock, I'll finish you in time like I did your mother and father. "*

"I'm ready," he screamed for Robert, "I am ready for you, Father Rock. I will kill you when next we meet." Don continued "Then all will be mine! Everything that exists will be under my power. I will rule with the dark forces." Don's body exploded with a dark light that streamed towards the heavens as the cult members moaned in ecstasy. The body, no longer Demos, slumped to the floor dead. The cult offered a solemn prayer and burned the body in a ritualistic ceremony. The body was a mere earthly vessel. The ashes were carried to the four corners of the earth to be scattered to the winds. Demos would be born again at the proper time. The cult would be ready.

The viewer next showed Robert at the age of seventeen. *Robert's image changed to Father Rock. He began having visions of dimensional objects, colors of energy fields and automatic writings of quantum math symbols that were advanced formulas for antigravity and time travel. He was asking questions, "Who am I? What is my mission?"*

The team experienced it all as if they were there with Robert as his memories came flooding back. They were amazed at the visions of universal understanding.

The viewer showed Robert hearing the familiar voice "YOU WILL SOON UNDERSTAND YOUR BEGINNING TO THE NOW OF YOUR EXISTENCE." The viewer showed Robert standing on a mountaintop with his hands stretched up to the sky. The voice spoke. "ROBERT, YOU ARE FATHER ROCK, SENT FORTH TO DO BATTLE WITH DEMOS AND HIS DEMONS. THIS WILL BE THE BATTLE THAT DECIDES IF GOOD OR EVIL FORCES WILL CONTROL ALL EXISTNG THINGS. THIS BATTLE WILL TAKE PLACE A TRILLION LIGHT YEARS IN THE FUTURE ON A PLANET NOT YET BORN, CALLED EARTH." The authoritative voice spoke for hours, preparing Father Rock for the battle and telling him of his mission.

"TEAM," the voice said, "YOU KNOW THAT FATHER ROCK CANNOT BE TOLD ABOUT HIS PARENTS AND LOSING THE BATTLE TO DEMOS, THE KNOWLEDGE WOULD WEAKEN HIM." The voice said, "I AM NOW GOING TO TAKE HIM OUT OF HIS TRANCE." A high-pitched sound wailed and a flash exploded on the screen.

Eight

Father Rock opened his eyes and said, “We are running out of time. I’ll have to call the Muzoids to help us before long.” “Muzoids,” said Dr. C, “what’s a Muzoid?” Zoron said, “You’ll find out soon enough. Let’s just get the final phase of the time transporter work done.” They worked tirelessly until the time transporter was finished. Father Rock said, “Great work! Now I will program the time transporter to bring it to a functional state.”

Father Rock typed “I am the” on the keyboard and then keyed in some quantum symbols. Fast-running quantum math equations scrambled across the screen. When the calculations were complete, Father Rock said, “The time transporter is ready. Team Leaders, are you ready to travel?” Everyone said, “Huh?” Dr. C shook his head. “I have a feeling we're not. Not at all.”

Father Rock laughed and said, “Pack your bags. The time

transporter is ready to take us to the dimensional headquarters located in the middle of a black hole. It is called the Galtor Dimension. There, I'll tell you more about Demos, his demons, the Muzoids and how they will help us prepare for battle. Also, you shall see and learn how to operate the Digimoid computer built by the Muzoids. Zoron, you will develop my weapon, the sonic cyber guitar."

"We will be safe in the Galtor Region. Several trips will have to be made between Earth and Galtor to find certain crystals Zoron will need." Father Rock entered his code into the time transporter. "Oh yeah, get ready for the best light show in the universe. My friends, you will see yourselves traveling in the form of light energy through space. The colors you see and speed at which you will travel will amaze you. Don't be afraid, you'll come back to your human form on the Galtor Region Launch Pad, close to my dimensional home." Father Rock hit a key marked with a quantum symbol. The room turned color, a pretty blue. Metallic flakes streamed out of the viewing screen and floated in the room like confetti in a snow globe. Small red sparks of energy flared here and there.

Dr. C looked at his arm; it was blue and transparent. Dr. C said, "My word, I can see through my arm." Zoron and Jean echoed, "So can we." Their voices sounded faint and in slow motion. Suddenly there was a white flash, and then they were all gone. The room returned to normal and the time transporter was not visible. Now the Team Leaders took the form of energy flying through space and dimension, traveling at the speed of light. Stars flashed by, and colors more vivid than the mind could comprehend were surrounding the team. Bright blue, pink, violet, orange and red hot. It was endless. There were sounds never heard before, high frequency, like masses of birds singing. Then the wind was whistling through the trees, with a flute playing in the distance. Mixed in were very high crackling sounds like crumpling paper only a thousand times louder. High frequency blips like the ones used in a hearing test wove in and out of this mass of cosmic sound. They felt the rumbles of low frequency sounds like big bells that vibrated them even in their current form of pure energy. In front of them was a white tunnel of energy. They were sucked into the tunnel. It was as if they were in a white-hot storm but it felt cool and restful. As they sped through the tunnel, it changed colors and Jean began to change into her true form.

The trip through the time tunnel was incredible as colored lights and sounds became more and more intense. The lights started to flash very fast. The blip tones tapped in a repetitive pattern, like some kind of code. Dimensional designs and colors flashed by with everything swirling all at once. It was like touching heaven. A new low sound swelled and faded. It sounded like a big bell and the team vibrated with it. All at once with a loud cracking sound they found themselves back in their bodies, staggering on shaky legs.

Father Rock said, "Welcome to Galtor, my home." Father Rock's home was very unusual in design. Father Rock asked, "Zoron, do you feel a closeness to this place?" Zoron said, "Yes, Father Rock, I feel like I've been here before." Father Rock explained, "You have. This was your home before you were Zoron on Earth. Our meeting was not coincidental."

Zoron felt Jean stagger at his side and turned instinctively to offer support. He was transfixed in amazement by what he saw. The Jean he knew was gone, transformed into Aura, Father Rock's grand-daughter. Aura was beautiful, with long blond hair with blue eyes that penetrated one's soul. Aura had very creamy white, smooth looking skin. She was as exquisite as Venus, the goddess of love and beauty. She was dressed in a long flowing robe with specks of gold woven into the white fabric. She radiated both dynamic energy and a soothing calm.

Dr. C lost his battle with rising nausea and threw up on the smooth surface of the landing disk. To his amazement, the mess shrank and disappeared almost instantly. "My word!" he exclaimed, forgetting to be embarrassed over his indiscretion. Father Rock chuckled, "Ah, yes, I vomited so many times when I was a child that my father developed a highly efficient biological organism to break down organic waste. He was a very practical being. It's terribly efficient. The bacteria are specifically designed to consume human waste products. It eliminates accidents, dead skin cells, oily secretions, shed hair and the need for…ahem, most plumbing. Unfortunately, if I released it on earth, forensic science would be a lost art…and we'd never be able to figure out who dunnit!"

He pointed to a low rise a short distance away. "We'll just need to hike over in that direction to the compound. Can everyone walk?" Nodding uncertainly, the team followed Father Rock's retreating form.

Topping the rise, the team was surprised to see a gentle slope leading into a lush protected valley at the foot of a pyramidal mountain range. Father Rock led them down into the valley. The path led into the towering vegetation, like nothing they had ever seen before. The plants were mostly pastel colored with flashes of bright colors here and there. Zoron stopped to examine a plant growing close to the path, a stalk culminating in a cluster of hairy pink bulbs of varying sizes at the top. In contrast to the pale yellow of the thick stalk, a vine climbed up and around the plant, clinging to the meat of the stalk with tiny barbed hooks. Dotting the vine, tiny bright blue berries nested inside pairs of leaves with fringed edges that opened and closed at random. The effect was one of constant fluttering motion, both beautiful and startling. Zoron grasped one of the leaf clusters and tried to pull it off to show Aura. The entire plant shuddered and all the leaves snapped shut and curled inward. Father Rock took Zoron's elbow and guided him gently back a few steps, and then stroked the vine and spoke softly to it until the leaves began to flutter as normal. He turned to Zoron with a smile. "You were trying to pull off an eye stalk! Scared the poor thing nearly to death. I should have warned you that some of the animals here are quite different."

Zoron stammered an apology, but Father Rock waved it off. "It was hardly your fault. How could you have known? I should have paid more attention to my guests. No harm done, see? It's already feeding again." For the first time, Zoron noticed the pulsing of the barbed hooks and the minute milking action of the delicate vines. He shuddered. "Fascinating," he muttered, "simply fascinating."

A few paces further, and the path opened onto a large clearing at the foot of the mountains. Directly ahead, they saw a door cut into the mountain itself. Father Rock went to the door and touched it in a specific pattern. The door slid silently aside. "Welcome to my home." He said simply, ushering them into the cave.

The massive cave was filled with pyramidal structures of all different sizes. Scattered everywhere were small, medium, and large pyramids of all different colors. Placed at regular intervals were transparent tubular devices that appeared to have different crystals frozen in them to emit harmonious sound frequencies and colors of blue, red, black, purple, and green to keep the energy level within the human mind frequency capabilities. Blue energy orbs crackling with white-hot strings of energy moved inside the tubes filled with different color liquids, allowing the thought processes necessary to keep their energy in balance. This balance allowed their creative energies to function. Father Rock explained the functions of all these strange devices as he showed the team around.

Concluding the tour, Father Rock led the team into another room and went over to a series of circular discs. Father Rock waved his hand over them and as he waved his hand over the discs, they changed to different colors. As he moved his hands the walls changed colors and maps appeared of locations on Earth where the battle would take place. The various locations for the disbursement of the team were designated by color code.

Father Rock waved his hand again and a table came up out of the floor with food and drinks. “This meeting shall take several hours, so let’s eat, and then we can start fresh.” After a fine meal they began. Once everyone had their orders as to methodology and battle strategies, Father Rock said, “Let’s rest. We can start in the morning on the use of the Muzoids' code books.”

Nine

The next day everyone was up and ready to work. Father Rock kept all his code books in a secret room. The entrance to this room was behind a large angelic looking painting he had created it during one of his trances.

"This painting conceals an eye identification security system. I am the only authorized person to enter." Father Rock explained, "Come in but do not step on the blue squares or you will trigger the sentry device." The painting swung aside, revealing a small room lined with shelves and recessed drawers. Father Rock crossed the room to a locked cabinet and withdrew a stack of slim books. He gave one each to Zoron, Aura, and Dr. C. "This mission is on a need-to-know basis only. You three shall carry these top secret code books. Keep them close, never let them out of your sight." Father Rock then started to teach everyone the codes. This session was eight hours long with a three hour practice period, in total eleven hours of high concentration. At the end of the session, everyone was burnt out. Father Rock said, “Okay, let’s call it a day. I will be in my sanctuary for three days then we shall begin work again.”

Father Rock held his arms out in front of him and strings of white-hot energy came from his hands. A sound like chimes rang as an opening to a private chamber showed in the wall. This room was specially designed to be restful, a place of peace and comfort and tranquility; a sanctuary where one could return to his or her inner self. The celestial sound of Father Rock's guitar greets a visitor as he walks into the sanctum, a sound of universal music of balancing vibrations a constant of the all. There was a white light that turned to a soft blue color. One feels warm as this white light touches him, energized. And then the blue light shines upon him; he feels cool, relaxed and this light makes one feel as if in a good place with lots of energy. The mind, body and soul take in this positive force of energy and love. Scents flow through the room on gentle currents, sweet and softer smells like flowers, the rose and lavender. Some of the delicate perfumes have the scent of the ocean or a smell of strawberries. The room is filled with great love awareness and tranquility.

These scents bring new life to you and you are thankful to receive them. You feel everything around you to be alive and full of kindness and love. You are refreshed and energized. This is a place from which one may travel the universe with out-of-body travel to see the stars, galaxies and other dimensions of other places. You become one with the universe and travel in the form of light. As you look around Father Rock’s sanctuary you can understand more about Father Rock’s sanctuary and Father Rock himself. You can see his art of dimensional designs, a form of math with structural integrity and design never seen before. The magic writings of Father Rock are etched into the stone of the walls; coded formulas for harmony and balance. In the center of the room, a bed levitates two feet off the floor, rocking ever so slightly with the room's natural air currents. Star fields glow on the ceiling, providing gentle ambient light. This star map represents a real time view of the ever-changing universe, with stars twinkling and occasionally flaring out.

Father Rock believes everyone can find peace here, because we are part of all things. Because you already know all that exists, all you have to do is call upon this light of love. There you will find the you of yourself. As you look into the mirror of life, you can see your inner self and you will have this peace. (Ask and you shall receive.) The sanctum provides a focus for natural inner balance. Near Father Rock's bed a poem is printed on the wall. It reads…

> *Changing mass of life to transform into that which is unknown to be part of the magic of life, sometimes I wonder and remember you in a different form and you say to me and I say to you, but we don't hear; it doesn't matter because we have traveled in the same light beam before we came here. This feeling is genetic, from the center of the universe to infinity, before time was time before you took your human form. We are all what is called energy, an ever changing mass of life.*

FATHER ROCK

Father Rock relaxed on his bed and all around him glowed blue energy. A soft breeze blew through the room, fresh and clean, like the air after a rain storm, the scent of renewal. As Father Rock slept, he dreamed he was a free spirit at one with himself. Father Rock dreamed of his mother and father when he was a boy of about nine years old. The place they were in was in the woods. No, it was a garden. He saw his beautiful mother laughing. His father chased him around a tree playing tag. They were so happy. There was a songbird singing and doves in the tree. There was a blanket on the ground with lots of food, for a picnic.

Father Rock dreamed of his unicorn, a big white animal. It danced on its back feet, a majestic sight. Father Rock ran and jumped on Light Force. He was named Light Force because he was so beautiful and so fast. He could run to the speed of light. Sometimes they jumped dimensions in the form of pure energy. That's how Atom (Father Rock was called Atom as a boy) found the Muzoids. In hyperspace both Light Force and Atom did not like to make the jump. They always vomitted after the jump but they did it anyhow. They thought it worth getting a little sick just for the adventure.

In Father Rock's dream, Atom said "Ready? Here we go!" They landed in a dimension called Muzoid. It was a strange place. Big creatures, including one at least 20 feet tall, grazed near the spot where they landed. The land was rocky and had irregular protuberances almost like trees but huge, 300 feet or more, and purple in color. They heard a noise, a faint little sound like a small voice. Atom said, "Hello, anyone out there?" There was a faint response. Now they just had to find it, after all, a 9-year-old boy must look into everything he hears and sees. Light Force started walking and Atom had a good view from the unicorn's back. "There… it's over there," Atom said, pointing to a flower. In the flower was a cute little fuzzy-looking thing. It had fallen off a low cliff right into the sticky flower. Struggling had only tightened the petal prison around him. The little thing was shivering with fear. Atom realized he could read its mind. Atom projected a thought to the creature. "What is your name?" The creature's mind answered, "Spark. Are you going to hurt me?" Atom said, "No, I won't hurt you." "Can you get me out of this flower? It is poison and I will die if you don't help me." Atom nodded as he carefully peeled back each petal and lifted Spark out of the flower.

Freed, Spark busied himself by cleaning the residue from his fuzz. When he was satisfied, he looked inquisitively at his rescuer. "Where are you from and what is that you are riding?" Atom answered, "This is a unicorn and I call him Light Force. My name is Atom. I am from Galtor, far, far away from here in another time and dimension." Spark said, "You saved my life. Some day I will return the favor. Take this Digimoid computer and put in this code when you need me, and I will come." Atom said, "Thank you." Spark continued, "We are great warriors. I have 4 brothers: Zap, Tink, Zon, and Electro. Don't let our small size fool you. If you ever need anything just use the Digimoid and we will come running. Thanks." *Spark ran away, zip, so fast you could barely see him.* Atom laughed and scratched the base of Light Force's horn, saying, "Well we have some new friends, the Muzoids. We had better get home to mom and dad or they will worry." He swung up on the unicorn's back and braced for the gut-wrenching trip home. "Light Force, it's time to, oh! Here we go, Light Force." They made the jump. *Bam!* They landed in a clearing designated as the takeoff spot on Galtor, a safe distance from the garden and any obstacles they might land inside. "I hate to make the jump," Atom said. As always, the jump made them puke up their guts.

Atom's father, Alpha, and mother, Omega, were wonderful to him. Atom's life was protected from the vicious war that his father was fighting with the evil Demos. Alpha spent as much time as he could with Atom. They often played games. Alpha taught Atom the secrets of the universe, preparing him for his future role as the Ruler of the Universe. His father told him, "If something ever happens to me, Atom, you are to protect your mother from Demos." Atom solemnly promised he would.

Omega loved the Celestial Gardens at their home on Galtor. Atom loved his mother so much. He liked to watch her feed the animals. She would sing a pretty song to the birds. *Pretty birds come to me, pretty birds*. She talked to them and they understood her. Over 150 species of animals including gifts from friends in distant dimensions lived in the Garden.. Alpha and Omega were gentle souls and beautiful spirits with great cosmic powers. They ruled the balance of all things that existed with their positive frequencies and vibrational forces to infinity. Alpha told Atom, “Remember, I am always with you. We are as one and we shall always be as one frequency.”

Father Rock rolled over and continued to dream. Atom and Light Force were almost home when they heard screaming. Atom shouted, “Hurry!” and they hit full stride. They topped the rise and could see the valley now. Alpha was calling, “Atom, here, here.” “What’s wrong, dad?” “Demos has defeated our army. He’s coming to kill all of us.” Alpha said, “Get in here.” He waved his hand and a time chamber appeared. Alpha said, “You are quite young for this but I must transfer all my mind power to you right now.” Alpha placed his third eye to Atom’s third eye and blue energy filled Atom’s body. Atom shook and trembled and he fell limp. Alpha said, “Atom? Atom, are you all right?” Atom came out of a daze. “I said, are you okay?” Atom said, “Ya, ya, I think so.” “Atom, we do not have much time. I must get to your mother.” He gave his son a big hug and said, “I love you, Atom.” Atom said, “Dad, I love you too.” Alpha said, “Watch from here. If all goes bad this time transporter will turn you into white energy. You shall travel for one million years then you shall find a living capsule for your energy. Atom, Demos might follow you. If so, you will have to face Demos and kill him. Do you understand?” “Yes father, yes,” Atom said.

Alpha ran to get Omega. Demos flew around in a purple robe. Atom saw his father fighting this terrible creature. Atom’s father yelled, “Demos, you and your demons get out of my home. Go to your evil darkness.” Demos’ red eyes lit up and a black beam shot out. The beam of light hit Alpha and knocked him down. Demos landed next to Alpha, his purple robe snapping with energy. He said, “Now I shall rip your heart from your body." Demos clicked his 8 inch fingernails and jabbed them into Alpha's chest and grabbed his heart in his hand and crushed it, killing him instantly.

Atom watched in horror as Light Force lowered his head and charged at Demos, trying to kill him with his horn. One of Demos' demons, a flying serpent, wrapped itself around Light Force, and crushed him instantly to death. Atom saw his mother running with Demos right behind her. Demos laughed, "Ha Ha," saying, "Now join your husband." Demos fired a red beam and it missed her as she dodged behind a tree. Another big blast burned the tree to the ground and killed Atom's mother. Atom screamed. Demos, stopped, "What was that?" A songbird made a sound to cover up for Atom. Crying as he pushed the time transporter button, Atom declared, "I swear I will kill you someday Demos." Atom shot out of the time transporter. Demos said, "No! The brat got away. I must kill him too." Demos projected himself into purple energy to chase Atom's energy trail. But now Demos was thinking to himself, "I, the great and wonderful Demos am the Ruler of the Universe."

Bam! Father Rock awoke from the dream wringing wet with sweat. He was breathing hard and could barely catch his breath. The same dream of Demos haunted him every night. Father Rock sat on the edge of the bed and said, "That dream, that darn dream." He held his head in his hands while looking at the floor. It took a great deal of effort for him to even get up. He got out of bed slowly, stood a moment and walked over to the table and sat down. He waved his hand and a cup of herbal tea appeared. This tea would put him back to sleep fast. Father Rock looked out of the big pyramid shaped window that overlooked a garden. In the garden were beautiful white gold statues. The trees in this garden have black trunks, highlighted with precious gems; ruby sapphires, diamonds and emeralds. The leaves of the trees are gold. As a gentle breeze blew the leaves, the leaves acted as chimes and played a sweet soft song. This sound touched the soul and warmed the heart and spirit. He began to get sleepy again. As he sat in this gold chair, he looked over this place of beauty. His eyes gazed upon this awesome gift of life and he looked up and said, “I wish I was given more time with my parents. They were so good to me. I miss them so much.“ He lay down again and he drifted back to sleep. With inner peace the light became dim and he fell into a deep sleep.

Ten

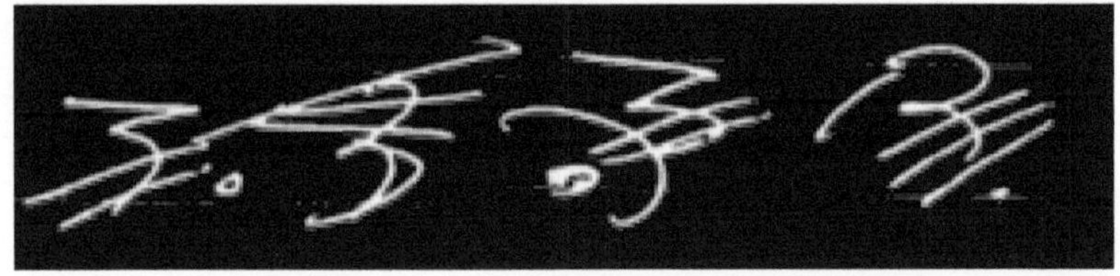

Emergency! Emergency! An urgent message flashes on the screen of all Digimoid computers. *Alert! All Muzoids report to the dragon valley dimension!* Reacting quickly, the Muzoids tapped a code into their digis, disappeared and re-appeared instantly in the dragon valley dimension. Tink said "Zon, go to the ridge of the rock and see what we are up against. Father Rock's message said they are on the move now." Zon replied yes sir. As Zon crawled up to the top ridge of the rock, he heard a loud hissing sound. At the top, he was shocked at what he found. On the floor of the valley was a big dragon statue that looked to be solid gold with black crystal eyes. A black beam of energy scanned back and forth across the entire valley area. Zon thought *it must be like a radar system.* A deep moat surrounded the dragon statue. In the moat, Zon could see some movement but he could not make out the cause. The hissing sound was coming from that area. Zon looked to the right edge of the valley. He saw a large walled area around what looked like huge eggs, at least 9 feet around. A fierce dragon guarded the eggs. He was black, shiny black, with thick scales all over his body like a heavy armor. A stripe of bright red scales ran down the center of his back and his wickedly pointed nails were three feet long and bright yellow. His teeth were cobalt blue and he had bilious green spears that stuck out from the back of his feet like spurs. As Zon watched, the dragon stood and spread his wings to an incredible 200 foot span. *What an awesome dragon*, he thought. Razor sharp bony barbs lined the underside of the dragon's impressive wings. *Those would cut someone to pieces. One swipe of that dragon's wing alone would reduce an enemy to ribbons.* The thought made Zon a little queasy. *These dragons are gonna be tough to beat in battle. That one alone is a flying arsenal.* ROOOOAR! The dragon made a deep booming sound and opened his mouth wide. A ball of flame shot from his throat, scorching the underbrush for a hundred and fifty feet. *Uh oh, that's going to be hard to deal with in battle.* Zon reluctantly tore his attention away from the yawning dragon and continued his surveillance. Pits covered the floor of the valley, deep holes. *That's probably where they sleep.* Zon hit the dirt as a dragon flew low overhead. The dragon sailed into the valley, circled, and landed atop the gold dragon statue, where he began beating his wings, producing a loud, rhythmic clicking noise. All at once, dragons began to rise from the pits in the ground. It was an awesome sight. Each dragon was unique and colorful. Some flew, some crawled, some slithered, and a few rolled their bodies up and rolled like giant scaly balls. Zon made a quick count, but lost track at eighty. *This is unbelievable! I gotta get this info back to Tink right now!* Watching the skies to be sure he wasn't spotted by flying dragons, he hurried back down the ridge to tell Tink what he'd seen.

Tink started programming battle strategies into his digimoid computer. After he'd run every possible scenario, he turned to the Muzoids. "Ok, guys, listen up. We are greatly outnumbered. I have programmed your digis with D.T. programs. Each one of us has a different weapon programmed in. Here's the plan. We shall spread out to form a complete circle around this valley on the top of the ridge. We will begin our attack together, all at the same time. We must catch them off guard. This is the only chance we have. Now let's get ready to fight." The Muzoids stacked their hands together and did their famous battle cry, "WIN! WIN! WIN!" Tink entered a few fast codes into his digi. "Ready?" The Muzoids nodded. "This will send us to our posts around the valley. Each of you check in with me once you're in position and ready to attack. We begin on my signal." Tink pushed a button and ZAM! The Muzoids were disbursed. In moments, the reports began coming in. "Zon, ready and on standby." "Spark, ready and on standby." "Zap, ready and on standby." Tink waited for Electro's report. A minute passed, then two. Tink began to worry. *What could have happened? Could I have miscalculated?* He sent a message to the others to sit tight until he figured it out.

Electro was in big trouble. He'd materialized in the middle of a dragon demon's den. He was surrounded by dragons but they had not spotted him yet. He was on a shelf-like stone overlooking the den. Below him, three dragons were tearing apart an animal they had killed. They growled and snapped, fighting over the bloody chunk of meat. One dragon clawed another's side, cutting a big gash in him. While those two dragons fought, the third dragon dragged the carcass into a corner and began wolfing it down, leaving the others to battle. Electro thought, *I've landed at the gates of Purgatory. What am I going to do?* He looked at his digi and flipped rapidly through his programs, looking for a D.T. to help him fight his way out of the den. Electro spotted a D.T. called Powerforce and pulled it up. *Ok, let's see what we got here...*Powerforce: this dimensional transcender can melt stone and can turn water into metal 5 minutes after the subject has come into contact with the cosmic dust. *Hey, that sounds good,* Electro thought, keying in the code. *BAM!* A small packet of cosmic dust appeared, just one gram of dust in a cobalt blue bottle. In the center of the cave was a spring fed by volcanic activity. The water bubbled in places and steam arose, making the cave warm and wet. Towards the back of the cave, the water was calm and dark, and several times Electro observed dragons going there to drink. His problem was clear. How to get past the dragons to the water to dump the cosmic dust into the spring?

A second bottle appeared. It was red, and contained one gram of stone devac. A plan began to form in Electro's mind. *I can dissolve the stone in the cave,* he thought. Then he looked at the shelf below his feet. *Bad plan...what am I thinking? I must do better than that. I need another idea.* He began flipping through more programs. *There must be something here that can help me!* Across the cave, a dragon lifted his snout and began sniffing the air, scenting new prey. He was one of the two who had fought and missed dinner, and he was hungry. He walked towards Electro's hiding place. Quietly, Electro opened the blue bottle of dust and sprinkled a little on the edge of the shelf. He flattened himself against the cave wall at the back of the shelf, willing the dragon to go away. Clawed feet appeared on the edge of the shelf as the dragon followed the scent. Electro shook with fear and beads of sweat appeared on his forehead. The dragon's head appeared over the edge of the shelf, swinging blindly. *They must be blind,* Electro thought, *he's tracking by scent alone.*

There was a woosh of air as the dragon took a big sniff. He raised his head and groaned, as if he were in pain. *The powder must be burning his nose,* thought Electro. The dragon dashed across the cave to the cool water and dunked his head. He came up shaking and growling, and shot a ball of fire over the dark water. Then he lay down and appeared to go to sleep. A few minutes later, his heaving sides became still. Another dragon wandered over and began pushing the dead dragon with his nose. Realizing his brother was dead, the dragon began to make keening sounds. The other dragons came to investigate and their voices joined in an eerie death knell, which was soon replaced by angry, aggressive sounds. The dragons went nuts, spinning all over the cave, bouncing off the walls, snorting angry bursts of flame. Electro decided to take advantage of the confusion. *It's now or never.* He pulled out his sonic ray gun and shot one of the dragons. The dragon fell, killed by the power blast. Two dragons remained. He took aim and fired again, but nothing happened. The indicator on the gun flashed “No Power”. “Oh man, no power!” Electro screamed, panicking. He leapt behind a big rock for cover. *You have to calm down,* he lectured himself, *get a hold of yourself! Remember, they can't see, and the cave reeks of sulphur.* Electro took the stone devac from the red bottle and poured it onto a nearby boulder. A giant serpent demon, drawn by the sounds of the agonized dragons, slithered into the cave and wrapped itself around one of the remaining dragons. The snake serpent was the color of mustard and let off an odor so strong that it choked the air. Electro could hear the bones of the captive dragon crunching and snapping as the serpent demon began to devour it alive. The last dragon grabbed what was left of the bloody carcass that had been dinner and ran out of the cave.

This is my chance, Electro thought, dashing wildly from the cave. Finding, cover, he remembered the mission. *I have to report to Tink.* He snapped his digi open and sent the signal. “Electro, ready and on standby.”

“Well, it's about time. Knowing Electro, he was probably goofing off.” Tink grumbled, but he was relieved, and he knew that Electro was a serious soldier who would never shirk his duty on a mission. He sent a message to alert all the Muzoids that everyone was in place and ready. The next message, seconds later, signaled the attack. The Muzoids keyed up their various D.T.s. Spark stood up and grinned like he always did before a battle. He took off his sunglasses and wiped them with a cloth, then summoned Meltor. Meltor looked like a black diamond. He broke into a million small diamond shaped crystals, which flew through the air and landed all over the valley floor. Instantly, they began to heat up. In moments, the valley floor was red-hot. The gold statue began to melt. Some dragons were killed immediately and some made it back into their pits. Growling sounds of pain filled the air. Dragons ran and jumped, but there was nowhere to land. The entire valley floor was afire. The dragons that did not make it into the pits or into the air burst into flame as Meltor cranked up the heat. A few vibor demons began rising from the pits. Meltor had no effect on vibors. Electro called his D.T., Etor, a weapon designed to fight vibors. The vibors live in water and tunnel underground. Their battle method is to come out of the ground near the enemy, crush and eat them. Zon was not looking and missed the vibor coming up behind him. Seeing a moving shadow, he whipped around and stabbed the demon in the chest with his cyber wand. The demon exploded and Zon turned back to the battle.

He coded in his D.T., Sleeptor. A red and green light appeared and the vibratory frequencies of peace spread throughout the valley. The flying dragons still alive landed on the cooling valley floor and fell asleep under Sleeptor's calming influence.

The real trouble will be when the vibor demons start coming forth in great numbers. They normally live beneath the ocean, but had massed under the valley in tunnels for the battle ahead. Each vibor is about ten feet tall and weighs 500 pounds or more. Their bodies are mottled with sickly green and yellow, and their huge muscles make them look like body builders. Large fangs protrude from wide mouths full of big, pointed teeth. Tink knows that in the final battle, the Muzoids and the vibors will face off.

Ten above ground dragons were still alive. Tink summoned the Great White Dragon. He materialized from nowhere on the ridge, a magnificent creature of positive force. His eight heads gleamed snow white in the smoky sunlight, and his eyes sparkled like perfect diamonds. He stood ten times larger than any of the other dragons, a commanding sight surrounded by a light of positive energy so bright that looking at him for too long would cause a person to go blind. The valley began to fill with his presence in the form of bright light and strong wind. The black dragons sensed his presence. It made them nervous and sent them running around in circles. Through the haze and the light, the white dragon appeared over the valley, gliding in on his wide white wings, a spectacular sight to behold. As he flew over the valley, he shot out precise white hot beams of energy that killed the visible dragons. He landed on the spot where the gold dragon statue had been. He opened his mighty wings and slammed them together, causing a sound like thunder. The very earth shook at his command. The demon dragons hidden in the recesses of the valley pits rose as if summoned, into the bright light. They died instantly on exposure to the light. In moments, the valley floor was littered with dead dragons and only the Great White Dragon remained standing.

The Muzoids did their famous victory dance. Suddenly everything started whirling, the wind and the clouds circling faster and faster, and the Muzoids were sucked out of the dragon demon dimension.

Abruptly, Father Rock awoke and sat straight up. He thought, *I can't take this stress any more. Battles on every front! Everything seems to be surrounding me, absorbing me. I can't sleep, I can't rest.* After a few minutes, he settled down again. *I have to deal with this,* he thought. *I will face it. And I will win. The Muzoids will be fine. They fought in the second dimension at a different mental frequency. The two do not phase, so the Muzoids will have no memory of this battle. They did well, as I expected.*

He settled once more on his bed and consciously relaxed his body until he fell into a dreamless sleep.

Eleven

Pinpoints of light signaled a new message from the viewer on the wall and a familiar voice boomed, “TEAM LEADERS, THE TIME HAS COME FOR FULL DISCLOSURE. YOUR EDUCATION BEGINS NOW. FATHER ROCK IS THE RULER OF THE UNIVERSE. HE IS THE MOST DYNAMIC GUITAR PLAYER THAT EVER EXISTED. HE HAS ALWAYS BEEN AND HE WILL ALWAYS BE THE FORCE OF ALL GOOD THAT EXISTS. HE HAS GREAT PHYSIC POWERS. HE IS A PHILOSOPHER, A GENIUS OF MATHEMATICS, A PERSON WHO HAS COME TO EARTH TO DEFEND THE GOOD FORCES OF ALL EXISTING THINGS AGAINST THE EVIL DEMON DEMOS. FATHER ROCK’S WEAPON TO SAVE THE WORLD FROM EVIL FORCES IS HIS LASER GUITAR. IT SHOOTS LASER BEAMS AND ROCKETS AND CREATES THE SOUNDS OF THE UNIVERSE. SUPER HIGH FREQUENCY, SUBSONIC LOW FREQUENCY SOUNDS ARE SOME OF THE MIND-BLOWING TONES OF HIS GUITAR. HE SHALL USE HIS UNIVERSAL MUSIC TO DESTROY ALL EVIL, AND ALL THAT IS EVIL IN THE UNIVERSE COMES FROM DEMOS.” Then the voice went silent.

Dr. C said, “Zoron, I see the reason needed for you and Aura but I wonder if my job is done.” Zoron recalled that Father Rock had said Dr. C would be working closely with the Muzoids. The mysterious Muzoids again. "Haaa," Dr. C said, rolling his eyes. He fired up his pipe and puffed smoke furiously out of both sides of his mouth.

The voice came again. "NOW," continued the voice, "I SHALL INFORM YOU ABOUT THE MUZOIDS AND YOUR MISSION. TEAM, RELAX AND LEARN.

THE MUZOIDS ARE ENERGY ANIMALS. THEY WILL PROVIDE ASSISTANCE TO ZORON THE ENGINEER. THERE ARE FIVE MUZOIDS. THEY ARE NAMED: SPARK, ELECTRO, ZAP, TINK AND ZON.

MUZOIDS AND FATHER ROCK ALL WEAR BELTS WITH A SMALL DEVICE CALLED A DIGIMOID COMPUTER ATTACHED. ALSO ATTACHED TO THEIR BELTS IS A GOLD DEVICE THAT RESEMBLES A TEST TUBE AND CONTAINS TRILLIONS OF NANO CHIPS. NEXT TO THE NANO TUBE IS A WAND LIKE DEVICE. IT IS TOO COMPLICATED TO EXPLAIN THE NANO CHIPS' USE OR THE CYBER WAND EXCEPT THEY WORK TOGETHER IN BATTLE AND THEY ARE VERY DANGEROUS. THEY ARE USED ONLY AS A LAST-RESORT WEAPON. THE DIGIMOID COMPUTER ALLOWS THE MUZOIDS TO CALL HELPERS TO ASSIST THEM IN BATTLE. THESE HELPERS ARE FROM THE CYBER DIMENSION. THE MUZOIDS HAVE HUNDREDS OF CODES TO CALL THE ENTITIES FROM THE CYBER DIMENSION. THESE HELPERS ARE CALLED DIMENSIONAL TRANSCENDERS OR D.T.'S. THE D.T.'S HAVE UNBELIEVABLE POWERS.

ALL MUZOIDS, FATHER ROCK AND TEAM LEADERS WEAR THE UNICRYSTAL IN THE FORM OF A NECKLACE OR A RING OR BRACELET. THE UNICRYSTAL IS A COMBINATION OF FIVE CRYSTALS THAT SYMBOLIZE TEAM UNITED WORLDWIDE, AN ORGANIZATION CREATED BY FATHER ROCK TO PROTECT THE GOOD FORCES OF THE UNIVERSE FROM DESTRUCTION BY EVIL FORCES. THE BLUE CRYSTAL

PROTECTS THE SKY, THE GREEN CRYSTAL PROTECTS THE TREES, THE BROWN CRYSTAL PROTECTS THE EARTH, THE YELLOW CRYSTAL PROTECTS THE ANIMALS, AND THE CLEAR CRYSTAL PROTECTS ALL PEOPLE AND THE UNIVERSE. THOSE WHO WEAR THE UNICRYSTAL AND BECOME A PART OF TEAM UNITED WORLDWIDE ARE UNIFIED IN CARING AND LOVE. BY WEARING THE UNICRYSTAL THE WORLD SHALL SEE THAT YOU ARE PART OF THE TEAM THAT CARES ABOUT THE SALVATION OF OUR WORLD AND OUR UNIVERSE AND ALL EXISTING THINGS.

FATHER ROCK SOMETIMES GIVES THE UNICRYSTAL TO A PERSON HE FEELS IS PURE OF HEART. WEARING THE UNICRYSTAL IS A STATEMENT THAT YOU CARE ABOUT THE BETTERMENT OF THE WORLD AND THE UNIVERSE AND THAT YOU ARE PROTECTIVE OF ALL EXISTING THINGS. PEOPLE WHO WEAR THE UNICRYSTAL WILL BE THE ONES THAT LEAD THE WAY TO SAVE THE FUTURE OF OUR PLANET AND THE UNIVERSE FROM DESTRUCTION." The screen turned to black and the team sat in awe, trying to digest the information.

Dr. C said, "Now I understand. I've been selected to be part of TEAM UNITED WORLDWIDE for the betterment of the planet and the universe. I will proudly wear the symbol of TUW, the necklace. All the e-mails you got, Aura, before we left earth are from team members waiting for our direction as Leaders. We are here to serve Father Rock to fight Demos and save the planet from his evil doings. I am deeply honored to be part of TUW and even more to be selected as a leader of the team." Zoron nodded thoughtfully, "It is a great gift and responsibility. We must all do everything we can to expand TUW."

Zoron strode to the master computer. In a gold box with quantum symbols on the top inscribed in black bold letters were the words "CODE MUZOIDS." To open the box required a blue crystal to be placed against a blue button. Zoron took his unicrystal necklace off and placed the blue crystal in his necklace against the blue button on the box. The box opened and inside the box was a blue and gold book. On the book were the words "CODES MUZOIDS". Zoron picked the book up and opened it to the first page. The directions read, "To summon the Muzoid warriors, enter the following code exactly as shown: M+ZORON+ZM3=V+G=MUZOIDS." Zoron entered the code and said, "It's time we met the mysterious Muzoids."

On a stone receiving pad beside the computer the first Muzoid appeared: Spark. Spark looked like a ball of lightning, small hair like tentacles and electricity shooting in every direction. Sparks of energy highlighted a cute little face with a big smile, two squinting eyes and a little button nose. Aura said, "He's so cute."

Spark flew across the room to Aura and gave her a little shock on the cheek. Spark said in a very high voice, "You're not so bad yourself, baby" and he giggled. Spark zoomed all over the room like a fuzzy little pinball. Dr. C ducked and chuckled as Spark whizzed by, "The Muzoids seem to be very playful." Zoron said, "Father Rock warned me about the Muzoids. They are playful and they love to play tricks on you so watch out for the little games they play." Spark jumped up right in Aura's face. "Oh," Aura said, "You scared me." Spark just winked an eye at Aura and shocked her once again on the cheek. That was Spark's way of giving a kiss, a tingly little shock.

Now another Muzoid appeared: Electro. Electro looked like a lightning bolt, but all of the sticks are solid little beams of lightning. Electro ran around the room, up the wall and walked across the ceiling. Then Electro dropped from the ceiling and landed on his feet on the floor. "Hello," he said, "I am Electro. What do you want to do? Where do you want to go?" Electro was ready to go anywhere and do anything. Electro jumped into Dr. C's lap. "Well Doc, lets get this show on the road." Dr. C burst into a big laugh saying, "So you're Electro."

Now the next Muzoid came. Zap looked like a fuzzy ball with long arms and legs, a big smile, holding arrows in each of his hands. He jumped up in the air and when he did he bounced all over the room. He bounced off the wall and ceiling. He said, “My name is Zap. I’ll zap you or I’ll wrap you or I’ll spin you around and turn you upside down. ZAP, ZAP, ZAP. That’s my name.”

Here came another Muzoid: Tink. Tink said sarcastically, “Yeah, yeah, we are all cute and lovable and funny. We all have big smiles and charming eyes. Now what’s the job? Where do we do it and when do we get started?” Tink continued, “Yeah, I look like a furry little animal with sunglasses. Now hug me. Now squeeze me. Now see how great I am. I’m Tink, the greatest Muzoid of all, ha ha.”

Zon appeared. He looked like a little bodybuilder with wire for hair sticking straight up in the air. “I guess Tink told you how great he is. That’s BULL. I am the greatest.” All the Muzoids were wearing their belts with their Digimoid computer. Father Rock, now fully rested, joined the others in the computer room, “They are cute and playful and love to play jokes, but don’t underestimate the Muzoids. They are very intelligent and they are the fiercest warriors in existence. They can get serious real quick in battle.”

Twelve

"No one would ever want the Muzoid as the enemy in battle,"

Zoron said, “I'm glad they are on our side.” Father Rock appeared from the entry to his sanctuary. “I see you've met my friends." He grinned at the Muzoids. "Zoron", he said, “Its time to design my new laser guitar. It must be your greatest work. You will need some special crystals. Have a look at my design diagram.” Zoron nodded. “I studied it while you were resting. Father Rock, you will have to program the Time Transporter to send me and the Muzoids back to Earth to find the blue, red, and black crystals of perfect size to fit your guitar.”

Father Rock prepared the Time Transporter, entered the codes, and sent the Muzoids and Zoron to Earth to search for the crystals in a remote area of the jungle. They all knew this was the most dangerous part of the jungle. This was where the forbidden caves were located, the caves where

FATHER ROCK

Demos had put his evil statue idols of the golden lion. One statue had blue and red crystal eyes and the statue of the god of the rain forest, Rankin, had black crystals for eyes. Demos had stolen the crystals from Father Rock in the last battle when Father Rock was defeated. The caves are protected by a tribe of cannibals who called themselves the Rankin. Zoron knew they would make a nice meal for the tribe if they were captured.

Zon, Spark and Zap were not very happy about this trip to the caves. They told Zoron, "We will never make it past the spider bushes." Zon and Spark said, "One bite from the dangerous black and red spider and you are dead and there are thousands of spiders in the bushes." Zoron led the way. He lit a torch and used the flame to burn the spider webs out of the way and kill the spiders. Picking a path carefully between still smoldering bushes, they made it past the spider bushes without incident, leaving a black pathway of burnt spider carcasses behind.

The Rankin tribe had built a semi-circular snake pit around the entrance of the cave. Zoron grimaced; he hated snakes. "Okay boys, cut this tree. It will fall across the snake pit and make a bridge for us to get into the cave."

In the distance they heard the sound of drumbeats. Zoron said, "The drums signify preparations for battle. The tribe believes that they can not go to war until they pay tribute to the gods with a war dance. The tribe will charge us when the drums stop." The Muzoids cut the tree to the rhythm of the drums. It came crashing down. A perfect shot. The tree was now a bridge straight into the cave. "Hurry, hurry," said Zoron. "We must get the crystals and get out." They ran inside the cave. Deep inside grew a magical tree. This tree was special. The heavy fruits hanging from its branches were round and gold. The tree branches were gold and silver and the trunk of the tree was diamonds, rubies, and emeralds. The gold apples swung slowly, although there was no breeze. The leaves were touching, making musical chimes. At the bottom of the tree was a gold step.

Zoron's curiosity got the best of him and he started towards the tree. When his foot hit the gold step, the tree played a song of loud chimes. A burst of energy illuminated the cave, shining a beam of blue-white energy against a far wall. The light revealed an opening in the cave wall and a path was lit up to show the way down a winding path. Their footsteps on the path triggered a small boulder that fell and crushed a statue of a Rankin god. Hidden inside the statue was a blue crystal. Indian symbols painted on the boulder said, “The blue crystal is a healing star.” Zoron put the blue crystal in his pocket and said, “We must find the big crystals for Father Rock’s guitar.” As they went down the path hundreds of bats flew past them. Zap swatted at them wildly, “Bats! I hate bats.” Zoron said, “Knock it off, all caves have bats. Let’s go. Keep your eyes open and your mouth shut. This cave is a dimensional portal, where several dimensions collide. That's why the tree is there, and why there is ambient light with no apparent source. We must be very careful to stay within the confines of our own reality.”

Ahead they could see two large statues of a cat god with big black crystals for eyes. Spark started to run to the statue and Zoron grabbed him saying, “No, go slow, the Rankins surely set some kind of a trap. Rankin traps may not be very sophisticated, but they can certainly be deadly.” Zoron took his walking stick and poked the ground in front of them. After about twenty feet, the stick went down into the ground about a foot. “Trap,” Zoron whispered. The Rankin had put leaves over a pit. In the pit were sharp stakes sticking up. They edged carefully around the pit. They were now only about ten feet from the statue. Three steps led to a pedestal where the statue rested. Zoron noticed a thin piece of string drawn tight across the first step. Zoron tripped the string with his walking stick. As the string broke, a sharp blade was released. It swung back and forth in front of the statue in a wide arc, barely missing Zoron. As its swing slowed, Zap said, “Boy, almost got you, Zoron.” The blade finally stopped and they retrieved the crystals from the statue. They turned to leave the cave and found the pathway blocked by a huge, three headed snake. The heads weaved back and forth menacingly and the long tongue flicked in and out, dripping thick slime. Sharp spines ran the length of the pale yellow body.

“Don't move”, Zoron whispered to the Muzoids, “I can handle this.” He unscrewed the top and bottom of his walking stick, leaving only the hollow middle. Pulling a long pin from under the band of his hat, he put it into the tube. He lifted it to his mouth waited for the right moment. The snake drew back to strike. It opened the middle head's mouth to spit poison from its fangs, but Zoron was faster. He blew the pin into the snake's mouth. The pin pierced the roof of the snake's mouth and buried itself in the tiny brain. The snake dropped to the floor, limp. Zoron said, “Let’s get out of here.”

The Rankin were waiting outside the cave. As Zoron and the Muzoids ran out of the cave, the tribe charged. Adrenaline rushing, they ran hard. The spider bushes were just ahead. Zoron had left markers so he could find the path. If they could just get past the spider bushes they would make it back. The tribe would not enter the taboo ground between the spider bushes. Spurred by fear, they managed to slip between the still smoking spider bushes before the tribe caught them. Arrows whizzed past their heads. Zoron yelled, “We made it, boys, we made it. We got the red, blue and black crystals.” The howling tribe stopped at the edge of the spider bushes and watched Zoron and the Muzoids get away. Zoron said, “Boy I hate snakes and spiders. They give me the willies.” “And bats, don't forget bats,” added Zap. “Let’s get out of here.” Zoron pushed the Time Transporter crystal on his necklace and transported them all back to the launch pad on Galtor.

Thirteen

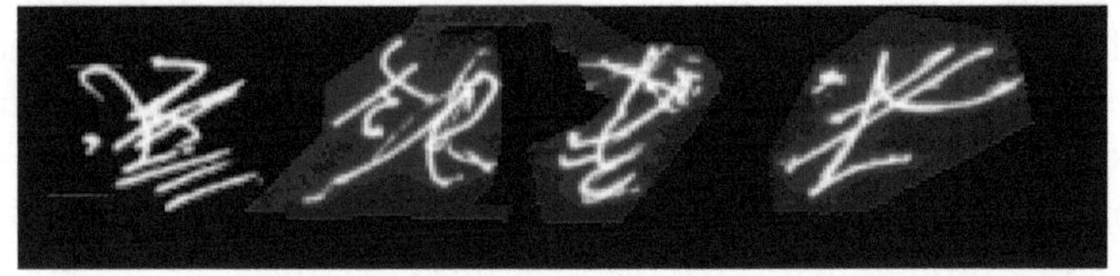

Zoron and the Muzoids walked wearily back to the compound. Dr. C walked out to meet them. "Did you get the crystals?" Zoron said, "Yes, and they look great. We must start the crystal testing process. The blue crystal first." They had gathered several blue crystals. Zoron placed a blue crystal in a pink metallic liquid. Then he started to send high-frequency sound into the pink liquid. As Zoron raised the frequency the blue crystal shattered. Electro said, "Oh no, one dead blue crystal." Zoron took another blue crystal and set the test up again. "Here we go," said Spark. Zoron programmed the frequency range again. The blue crystal survived the test. "That's a good one," yelled Zon. The testing continued. Red was next. Zoron set the red laser beam in the center of the red crystal. The red crystal reflected red beams all over the room. Zoron says, "Good, good, that's a perfect red crystal. Okay."

Spark was thinking, *It's been a very long day. Time to lighten this testing up. Time for a trick.* Spark took some sugar and made rock candy and put different color food coloring in it. The candy looked just like Zoron's crystals. Spark said, "Okay guys, each one of you; Electro, Zap, Zon and Tink, take one of the crystals (which we know are really rock candy)." "Okay." Zon took red. Tink took blue. Zap took yellow, Electro took green and Spark took the black crystal. "Ha, ha, rock candy. Hee, hee, hee, hee", he laughs. "Here's the trick," Spark said. "We will hold our crystal, well, really our rock candy, up and I'll say to Zon, these crystals can do anything. When Zoron is looking at us, I'll give you the high sign then I'll say, I bet they taste good too. Then we will all pop the crystal rock candy in our mouth. What a great joke." All the Muzoids agreed, "Yeah, yeah, ha, ha. Great trick."

Zoron walked into the room. Spark winked at the other Muzoids and said, "Hey, Zoron, these crystals can do anything." Zoron, Dr. C and Aura looked at the Muzoids. Zoron said, "Yes, they can." With that the Muzoids popped the rock candy crystals in their mouth. Zoron's eyes popped open. "No! No!," he screamed. Dr. C, muttered "My word, my word. Those little rascals." Aura's mouth dropped open. The Muzoids ran all over the room. Jumping, running, up the wall, down the wall, laughing, bouncing off the wall, acting crazy. They rolled all over the floor. Their eyes were rolling back and forth in their heads and they were making crazy noises. The scientists watched with their mouths agape. They had no idea what to do. Suddenly Spark stopped and said, "We fooled you! That wasn't the real crystals. That was rock candy. We made it to look like the crystals." Zoron growled and chased Spark as Dr. C swung his cane playfully at Zon and Tink.

Zoron said, "You Muzoids and your jokes." They all laughed and the joke really did break some of the tension of the testing process. Zoron said, "Okay, Muzoids, no more tricks. Now let's get back to work and test the black crystal." "Oh boy," said Spark giggled, "that was a good trick." The black crystal was the most critical crystal for Father Rock's guitar's power source. Zoron took the black crystal and placed it in Father Rock's guitar. There was no way to test black crystal but to actually have Father Rock use it as he played his guitar.

Zoron and Aura had been working very closely together. Dr. C noticed that their hands lingered when they touched. It was obvious to him that they were falling in love more each day. He often wondered when they would realize what was happening.

Zoron notified Father Rock that they had the first test ready. Father Rock stepped onto a circular disc that came up out of the floor in the center of this cave amid a structure of different colored pyramids. As Father Rock played, lights flashed. Father Rock played his guitar for about one minute. As Father Rock hit the last button to shoot the laser beam out of his guitar it shorted out. The black crystal exploded and an electrical shock hit Father Rock's arm and then bounced into his forehead, knocking him unconscious. Zoron, the Muzoids and Aura ran over to Father Rock, who was lying on the floor. They moved Father Rock onto a bed. Zoron got a wet towel and touched it to Father Rock's head as they tried to bring him back to consciousness. After about twenty tense seconds he finally opened his eyes. Zoron shined a flashlight into Father Rock eyes and asked him to follow his finger as it moved across his field of vision. After asking a few standard questions, he instructed Father Rock to wiggle his toes and stick out his tongue, Zoron announced, "Don't worry, he'll be all right. His eyes are focused and he does not appear to have a concussion. He will need rest."

The black crystal had failed to create the necessary energy needed to make the instrument work. Zoron and Aura labored hard to get the next test ready, but they needed to locate more black crystals before they could finish. "Now we have big troubles," said Zoron, "The black crystal is crucial, and difficult to find." Father Rock came back into the room. He was feeling better. He said, "Zoron and Aura, get ready. I will prepare the Time Transporter to send you back to Earth to find the black crystals. You must realize the black mountain range is very dangerous". Zoron nodded,. "We know, it's a dangerous mission but we are ready to go. Anything for the team."

They materialized at the outer edge of the black mountain range. Zoron said, "We must be very careful, Aura. We have to cross boiling springs and an active volcano full of lava on a rickety old swinging bridge." They knew this was the last place on Earth to get the black crystals. They also knew that Father Rock was counting on them.

After a grueling hike they arrived at the edge of a chasm leading to the black mountain. The swinging bridge was just ahead. As they approached the bridge Zoron said, "Look at the rope, it's broken." He bent over to pick up the broken rope and Aura yelled, "NO!" but it was too late. A snake bit his hand. It was the blue diamond snake. In a matter of hours, the poison would work its way through the system and the victim falls into a coma and sleeps forever. Aura would have to find a black mountain root to make an antidotal herbal tea before that.

Now Aura had big trouble. She had to get the black crystal for Father Rock and the black mountain tea for Zoron. Thinking fast, Aura rolled Zoron onto a sleeping bag and dragged it to a clear area protected by an overhang of rock. She made him as comfortable as possible and then started across the swinging bridge. Halfway over, one of the ropes broke. The bridge was hanging by one rope and Aura hung from that. She worked her way to the other side hand over hand, almost falling into the lava springs. Her hands were cut from the rough rope but she knew that she must keep going.

Aura wasted no time finding the black mountain root to brew the snake bite medicine. The plant's tender green shoots and delicate yellow flowers grew plentifully from the cracks in the rock, fertilized by the droppings of mountain goats. She filled a bag and hooked it to her belt. Now she needed to find a dull greenish rock. It was getting dark and she was worried about Zoron. Soon, she would have to give up the search and go back to him before it was too late. She was afraid the disintegrating bridge would not hold up for a return trip. She had to find that crystal NOW. Scrambling over a boulder, he saw a green rock. "Finally!" Aura ran over, picked up the rock and smashed it against the boulder. The rock broke open. She was lucky. Inside the hollow rock, crystals sparkled like black diamonds in the waning rays of sunlight. She almost cried from relief. "These are exactly what Father Rock needs to energize his guitar."

The bridge was even more frightening to cross back over. The wind had picked up and the rotting remains of the bridge swayed over the lava glowing in the distance below. The single remaining guide rope was darkened in places where her palms had bled, and she worried that it might be slippery from the twilight mist. She pulled on the hanging part of the bridge and dragged a piece up over the edge. Yanking a knife out of her belt pouch, she cut a long piece. She pulled the rope through her belt on each side of her waist and looped it over the top support of the bridge, tying the ends securely so that the loop formed a sling under her bottom. Gingerly, she lowered herself off the edge of the cliff. The first rope attachment was right in front of her. Careful not to cut the support, she cut the rope looping over it. The nearest part of the bridge fell away. Hand over hand, she pulled herself forward, sliding her rope along the support. She cut next rope attachment, making the bridge sway violently. She swallowed her nausea and kept going. After the third or fourth rope, it became easier. Her shoulders ached from the unaccustomed activity, and the circulation was cut off in her legs, but she did not pause. She could not pause. Zoron needed her. Everyone needed her.

It was getting very dark. Sobbing, she pulled herself forward to the next junction. Cutting through that rope, she put a hand forward and felt something brush her hand. It was a bush! She was on the other side! She grabbed the bush growing from a crack in the side of the cliff and pulled herself the rest of the way. It proved to be sturdy enough to climb up, and standing on it put the edge of the cliff at waist height. Cutting the rope that had formed her sling, she fell forward and wormed her legs onto solid ground. Face down in the dirt, she shuddered and lay still for a few moments, attempting to restore her balance. She was too weak to rise. On battered hands and knees, she crawled to where Zoron lay peacefully sleeping as she'd left him.

Fearing it was too late, Aura gathered some small sticks from nearby and built a fire to brew the black mountain tea in a canteen. She poured a small amount in the cap of the canteen and put an arm around Zoron to raise him to a sitting position. Placing the cup against his lips, she carefully poured a few drops into his mouth. She pleaded, “Zoron, Zoron, please wake up.” After a few sips of tea, his eyes fluttered open. Aura said, “You're awake! I was so worried!” She gently smoothed the hair back out of his face. “Are you strong enough to get home? I have the crystals.” Zoron said sleepily, “Yes, I’ll be fine.” He took her hand and pressed the torn palm to his lips. He grinned shakily. “Bet you've got some story to tell.”

Leaning on each other, they started back, but the trees lining the path were infested with strange-looking snakes. Zoron shuddered. “I've had enough snakes for one day. There is only one other way back to the dimensional transport point, through the Dark Caves. The Indian legends say the cave is haunted by spirits of the Star People. They say that the cave spirits have strong magic that plays tricks with your mind. People have reported strange things happening around the cave, floating balls of energy that can be seen for miles, and a strange red light with no apparent source that emanates from the cave at night, throwing shadows that have mysteriously independent movement. Are you sure you want to risk it?”

Aura looked into Zoron's eyes. “With you by my side, I can do this. Besides, we're scientists. The phenomena should prove fascinating.” She laughed nervously and squeezed Zoron's hand. “No time like the present.”

Fourteen

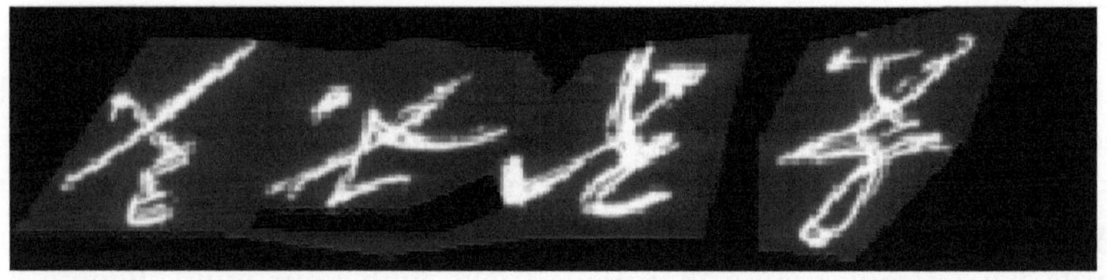

They walked into the dark cave entrance. “It’s black, I can’t see a thing.” Aura took two flashlights from her backpack and handed one to Zoron. When they turned the flashlights on, they saw a strange world. Green and yellow slime was coming out of a large crack on one wall. It was thick and had a sweet smell. The other wall had different colored stones laid in a pattern in some kind of message. The symbols were not

Indian. They were like something from another world, the language of the universe. The Indians called it the Star People marks.

The stories the Indians tell, say that a great fireball came to the village many, many years ago and the light spirits came from the fireball and floated in the air over to the dark cave. They went inside and they never came out, and the fireball zoomed away. The symbols were in three colors: red, blue and green. Aura said "Look up there," pointing to the roof. The cave had dots. These dots looked like star constellations. A map for space travel, at the end of the star field map was a large picture of a supernova's explosion. Zoron said, "Aura, looks like the space travelers had to run from their home place to Earth. It looks like their world is gone." Aura said, "Wonder what happened to the ones that came to this cave?" Zoron said, "I don't know, but they could still be waiting here for something. Right now we have Demos to deal with. We must get the black crystals back to Father Rock."

They started walking and they heard a strange sound like chimes. They did not know they were being watched. "You know, Father Rock had told me a long time ago about this legend of space travelers. I can't wait to tell Father Rock and Dr. C about this cave. Some day we shall all return to explore properly." As they went deeper into the cave the path narrowed and its roof slanted lower. Zoron and Aura were becoming very worried. Then in front of them the cave came to an abrupt end. There was a big symbol on the wall. It was a multidimensional drawing, like Father Rock's art. There was a small hole in the wall in an odd shape. Zoron said, "Wait a minute, I have seen this before. Father Rock gave me this gift." Zoron took the small metal device out of his pocket. Aura said, "Yes, it looks like it fits the hole in the wall." Zoron said, "Let's see if it fits." He put the device into the hole and a bright light melted the wall right before their eyes. Aura said, "Look, there is the transport point. Now we can get out of here. I hope Father Rock is feeling better." Zoron said, "So do I. We will tell him about the things in the cave after we take care of Demos and his demons."

They hurried to the Transporter, held their hands in the air and *ZOOM*! they were home, triumphant and very tired. Zoron asked Dr. C, "How is Father Rock?" "He does not feel that well at all, but you both need to rest. Your journey was most difficult." Zoron and Aura decided a picnic was just what they needed to relax and break away from everything.

The Muzoids were wonderful. They made a picnic lunch and gently shoved Aura and Zoron outside. They set off to an unexplored area to the right of the complex, drawn by a lovely natural glen on the banks of a small lake. Plants that were not quite trees and certainly not bushes grew on pale green stalks, with great bushy tops made of multi-colored leaves. There were a lot of pastel colored flowers in unfamiliar shapes, very exotic looking. The clouds scudding lazily across the sky were gold with purple and red tints around the edges of the clouds. The lake looked like a big pool of liquid metal. The color of the water was a deep, clear cobalt blue. It was as though they were looking into another time dimension. "It's absolutely beautiful and restful." Aura said, "I'm so glad we've taken time to be together and enjoy this getaway." Zoron picked a spot under a tall plant with golden leaves. The plant's sturdy trunk had an alternating diamond pattern with a reflective surface that created a prismatic effect of small light beams shooting in every direction. Zoron said, "This is the place." They spread their blanket and tried to relax away the physical strain involved in finding the black crystal and the nervous tension of the coming ordeal. They knew that time was running out and Demos was working just as hard to get ready for the impending battle.

They enjoyed the delicious meal. The Muzoids had fixed them fried chicken, mashed potatoes and gravy and their secret recipe, the Muzoid Pie. The Muzoids make many delectable and different sweets, but their specialty is the Muzoid Pie. They ate and then lay down on the blanket to rest. They were both so tired they fell into a deep and restful sleep. A couple of hours passed.

While Zoron and Aura slept, a bird landed in the tree and sang a gentle, pleasant song that slowly woke them. They sleepily admired the beautiful white bird. It resembled a dove, with gold rings around its creamy neck and lush iridescent tail feathers. Aura smiled at Zoron. “That is the most beautiful song I have ever heard.” If you can imagine all the stars in the universe being able to sing, that’s how they would sound."

Aura's brow creased. “I am very worried about grandfather. This has all been such a terrible strain. He is not looking well. Do you think he will be strong enough for this?” Zoron nodded. “Don’t worry, I’ll do all I can and so will Dr. C, the Muzoids and TUW. Father Rock has all the positive powers of the universe behind him. We will defeat Demos this time. He will be strong enough. He has to be.” Aura laid her head on Zoron’s shoulder and he wrapped his arms around her protectively. She put her hand on his cheek and raised her lips to meet his. Somewhere along the way, they had fallen in love.

They walked to the edge of the lake hand in hand and looked into the water. Their reflections were smiling and happy. A bubble broke on the surface, then another. All at once the water began to spin. It turned into a bubbling whirlpool. Before Zoron could pull Aura away, an energy creature reached up, wrapped itself around her and pulled her into the lake. The lake opened into a black hole. As Aura was pulled into space, Zoron saw vibrant colors, blue, green, dark-purple energy crackling around her receding form. Zoron could hear her screaming, but he couldn’t save her. In seconds, she had shockingly disappeared.

Fifteen

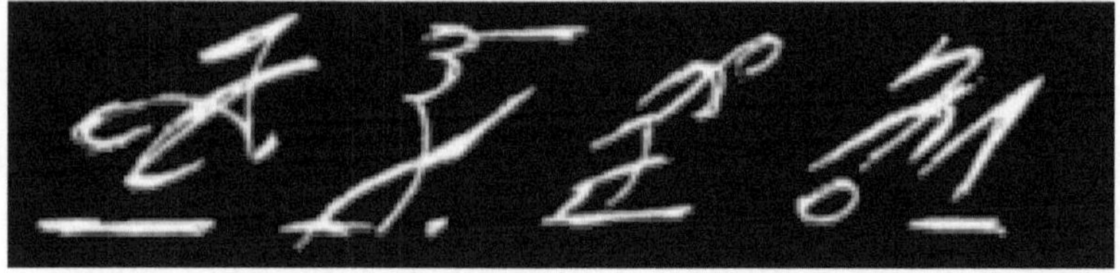

Zoron rushed to the cave where Father Rock and the Muzoids were working very hard to make the final battle preparations. Demos' voice was booming into the cave. "Father Rock, the only way you can ever get Aura back is to destroy me, but I shall destroy you. I have all the negative forces. I have the power of darkness; I shall defeat you."

All the activity in the compound had come to a stop with the first syllable of Demos' announcement. They stood motionless in a horrified tableau, the Muzoids at the computer, Dr. C at the table with a code book open in front of him, Zoron in the entrance with his mouth open to deliver the news. In the center, Father Rock crumpled slowly to the ground.

Aura slapped down on the ground in a mountainous area. *Boom!* She hit the ground hard. She came to her senses after a couple of minutes. All around her, black energy beams about one foot in diameter shot straight up to the sky. She moved up and touched one of the black beams and it made a vibrating sound and knocked her down. She was trapped.

Demos and his cult were laughing. Demos said, “Ah ha, Father Rock, I have Aura. I will destroy you, Father Rock. Now I’ve got the power. I have Zoron’s Aura.” Then Demos said he would make Aura his bride.

Demos soon realized that she was awake. “Pretty Aura, would you like a drink of water?” Aura's head snapped up. His voice came out of nowhere. She crossed her arms defiantly. “No!” “A little feisty, aren’t we? You’ll change your mind,” Demos said in his rough gravelly voice. “We’ll see, we shall see how hungry and thirsty you get. Oh, by the way, Aura, it gets cold here up in the mountains. If you change your mind just say, Demos, I need you.” He waved his black hand lazily in the air. “If you say you need me I will give you anything you want, of course, except your freedom.” Aura said stubbornly, “I’ll never say I need you, Demos.” Demos responded, “We shall see. You are mine, Aura, you just don’t know it yet.”

They converged on Father Rock's prone body from all corners of the room. Dr. C took his pulse and began issuing orders, "Zon, water! Spark, a blanket! Tink, smelling salts! Zoron, help me move him." Between them, they soon had him comfortable on a couch. Dr. C checked his eyes. Only the whites showed. "His pulse is strong, but his eyes have rolled back in his head. I think he may have simply overloaded from the stress." He pulled Zoron away from the couch, leaving the Muzoids to hover over Father Rock. "Zoron, this makes me very nervous. Do you think Father Rock is up for this? Can we win this battle?" Zoron ran a hand through his black hair, pushing it back off his forehead. "I don't know. Aura is worried as well. He needs to rest and recharge before this battle. Got to hand it to Demos. Kidnapping Aura was the best possible way to ensure that none of us will be at our best for the battle." Dr. C nodded. "There's only one answer. We must get her back immediately. Demos cannot be allowed to win the skirmishes."

In Demos' cave, the followers had gathered around the sacrificial table chanting "Demos! Demos! Demos!" On a big viewer screen they could see Aura on the mountaintop, shivering and cold. Demos sat in his king's chair made from the bones of bodies that Demos had defeated in battle. He laughed as he watched Aura on the screen.

Demos gloated with pride. He rose and held a staff in the air. "Father Rock, time is short." His voice filled the cave. In response, the cult chanted, "Demos! Demos! Demos!" "I am coming for you." The cult shouted "Demos! Demos! Demos!" "I will destroy you." The cult screamed "Demos! Demos! Demos!" Demos raised the staff above his head with both hands. The cult went crazy, dancing and throwing their arms in the air singing, "Demos the powerful demon, Demos the most powerful one."

Demos screamed, "Bring me the box I stole from Father Rock." One of the snake demons set his black box on the sacrificial altar. "Get back," Demos ordered. The demon bowed down to Demos and slithered away backward. Demos said, "I have one of Father Rock's treasures. Let me see." Reaching into the box, Demos pulled out a crystal skull and a crystal cross. When he picked the cross up, he did so with a piece of cloth around his hand. Demos hated crosses. "What's this?" Demos asked. It was a small red energy ball. Demos took it in his hand and screamed, "It burns, it burns."

Father Rock's image appeared in the room and he said, "Those of pure heart may touch the red energy orb. If you are not pure of heart the orb shall burn you and you shall get sick and have great pain." Demos screamed, "NO! NO!," his hands burning. Father Rock's image became more vivid and he said, "You may stop the burning by picking up the crystal cross." Demos said, "No, I won't touch a cross for anything." Father Rock said, "The pain will increase until you pick up the cross. You will die an awful painful death if you don't." Father Rock ordered Demos to pick up the cross to make the pain stop.

FATHER ROCK

Demos started making sounds like a wild animal. His robe was wringing wet from sweat. His eyes began to close and he screamed. Father Rock said, “Take the cross and the pain and sickness will stop all at once.” Demos grabbed the cross in his hands and shook it at Father Rock. “You think you’re smart. You fool! You should have killed me while you had the chance.” The demons were excited to see their leader back to full strength. They chanted "Demos will win in battle.” Upon examination, Demos found a holographic recorder that had projected Father Rock's message. “Good, so he still doesn’t know I took his box of gifts,” said Demos. "Soon, I will have it all. Everything that belongs to Father Rock will be mine!"

Zoron was very worried. The team on earth must be assembled by Aura. Her absence affected the entire operation. Father Rock had collapsed, Dr. C was pouring obsessively over the history files in the computer, looking for a similar incident in the past, and all work had stopped on Father Rock's weaponry. The team was falling apart. Zoron could not concentrate on anything else and had resorted to pacing in circles.

Tink called him over to where he was working. “Zoron, about Aura, I’ve been thinking,” as he tapped away on his Digimoid computer. “I’ve taken an intensity reading on Demos’ black beam that took Aura prisoner.” Zoron said, “What do you have, Tink?” “The power force of the black beams is low frequency and the beams extend one million three hundred thousand light-years into space. I have completed my calculations to send a high-frequency tornado just above the end of the black beams, generate a reverse energy and pull Aura’s molecular structure into my equation. If my calculations are correct, I should be able to pull her out the end of the black beam at one million three hundred and one thousand light-years, catch her with the Time Transporter and land her right on the Time Transporter Pad.”

Tink added, “Zoron, this is possible but there are dangers. We could lose Aura in the transfer." Zoron considered the warning for a moment. "What else can we do? We have no choice, let's try it. How long will it take you to get ready?" Tink said, "All I have to do is push this button on my Digimoid and in thirty seconds, if I am right, Aura will be back with us. If I am wrong…" He did not finish the sentence. "Okay," Zoron said, "Let's do it. Go ahead, Tink." Tink pushed the Digimoid button and everyone took a deep breath. Tink rolled his eyes. Dr. C said, "Ahhhhh," a big sigh. Zoron, anxiously rubbing his hands together, was almost in tears. There was a blue flash of energy and suddenly there was Aura.

The room erupted in shouts and congratulations. The Muzoids bounced all over the room like pinballs, shouting "Tink saved the day! Tink saved the day!". "You're all right Tink," Zoron let go of the grip he had on Aura to pat him on the back. Dr. C said, "Good show, right oh, good show, Tink." Aura hugged Zoron tight and didn't say anything. Zoron declared, "Demos almost took you from me. I was afraid before, but now I'm just mad!" Father Rock awoke to the commotion. He jumped up and announced, "We are ready to fight Demos now. We are all together. We must finish the weapons and get the mountain area ready for the conflict, the battle that will decide the future of all existing things from now to infinity."

Sixteen

Zoron and the Muzoids went back to work at fever pitch. Soon they were ready to put the black crystal in Father Rock's guitar. Zon took a pink liquid and submerged the black crystal in the liquid. "The black crystal frequencies will become stronger by using this method," he explained. Ten minutes passed. Zon took the black crystal out of the pink liquid and shot it with infrared light. "This", he said, "should do it."

Zoron said, "Let's try this new black crystal. We corrected some of the frequencies and the energy factors. We have your guitar ready, Father Rock." Father Rock examined the instrument carefully and nodded. "It must work this time. We are running out of time and Demos is about ready. I can feel it in the air, he is coming." Father Rock stood on the circular disc as it came up out of the floor to try the guitar again. Father Rock played a fast screaming run on his guitar. The Muzoids jumped up and down, saying "Yea, Yea, Yea."

Father Rock played a long burst of runs up and down the guitar neck. He put the guitar through all of its paces for speed, the color beams, sound intensity, and laser powers. Zoron had some tests set up for a demonstration of power including four red crystals. Father Rock spun around and ripped a high frequency guitar run that shattered all four of the red crystals.

Dr. C yelled, "Good show, Father Rock! Good Show!" Father Rock dropped to his knees and shot a laser beam into a three foot metal ball of solid steel and melted it. He jumped to his feet and screamed, "Demos, I am ready!" His voice echoed through the cave with great confidence and power. Father Rock let out a chilling loud scream like a wild animal and at the same time played some lightning guitar runs. The sound was awesome. Father Rock looked powerful as he played. He was connected as one with the universal power, deep in a cosmic trance.

He played the universal music of all existing things. The Team Leaders and the Muzoids were mesmerized by the performance. Gathering strength from the musical harmony Father Rock played on and on.

Back in Demos' musty old cave headquarters, Demos played his keyboard while his cult members jumped around. The serpents made discordant wailing sounds. Demos played wild, evil music as he prepared for battle. He said in his low, rough voice, "Father Rock is mine. I shall destroy you, Father Rock." The chanting cult was singing louder and louder, "Demos, Demos the great, Demos the powerful!" Demos played some powerful minor chords and low notes and he felt ready for battle. His long black fingernails ripped across he keys. His body twisted and crazy sounding moans came from deep in his chest. His eyes burned like fire in the darkness of his face. He played some more evil sounds on his keyboard and laughed. The echo created an eerie feeling around Demos. He screamed again, "I shall blow you away, Father Rock. The cult continued to chant "Demos, Demos, Demos."

FATHER ROCK

Father Rock played at full force. His white hair was electrified. It blew in the wind like spun stands of energy flying around in a blue energy field. Father Rock's hair changed colors, to blue, red, green and purple energy. His robe flowed gracefully. Father Rock appeared to move in slow motion. As he spun and turned and played his guitar with great emotion, laser beams highlighted changing patterns of colors. Father Rock played fantastic, out-of-this-world guitar runs. He screamed, "I shall send you back to the dark forces. I shall destroy you, Demos!"

Laser beams flew from the end of Father Rock's guitar. They flashed out an array of colors of the light spectrum. Father Rock's hair looked gold and a white blue energy field surrounded his entire body. He turned and shot two energy beams out of his eyes and hands. Father Rock was in a trance of other worlds and other dimensions. He was ready to face Demos in battle.

Tink said, "I want to ask you something. When Father Rock was playing his guitar, I saw an energy field of blue-white energy around his body. I then saw a force of shooting light beams come from his eyes and hands. Did you see this?" "Yes," answered Electro, "I saw the white-blue energy beams but I also saw electricity generate from his mouth when he screamed and lightning shot from his forehead." Spark said, "I saw all of those things but I also saw sparks flying out of his body in every direction, in every color you can imagine." "Then each one of us has seen Father Rock in a different energy image." "Dr. C, what is your hypothesis on this observation?" asked Zoron. "Well," Dr. C answered, "The way Father Rock explained it to me was, as the one cycle energy force that determines our capability of understanding is limited by the human capsule or by the captive vessel containing the one cycle energy force, the answer is yes. He says we can all see Father Rock in different images depending upon the date of our birth, place and time and how many dimensions we as individual energy sources conceive and/or function in."

"Gee Dr. C, couldn't you have just said, yes?" said Tink. Dr. C looked shocked, saying "Well I was sure you would want to know and understand why." "Okay, Okay, Doc. Thanks." Zoron observed, "Father Rock probably doesn't realize how he is perceived when he is playing his guitar. His physical energy appeared different to each of us."

"Although Father Rock is very muscular his whole body got larger and he seemed to be eight or nine feet tall in my mind's eye." Dr. C said, "By golly you're right, Zoron. Father Rock is hard to focus on with all the energies happening when he is playing his guitar." "His clothes changed," Tink said, "like shimmering diamonds with thousand of sparks and colors." "Perhaps Father Rock puts us all in some kind of cosmic trance of peace and tranquility, so powerful a spell our minds could not digest or comprehend all of this energy." Zoron said, "If that is the case and we all see Father Rock in different images just think of the energy he is emitting that is beyond our capability of understanding." Spark nodded. "This is the reason Demos must kill Father Rock. Father Rock is the teacher of good. Only then he will be able to unleash his dark frequencies of discord and unbalance on this dimension and dimensions beyond."

Seventeen

"Okay, Father Rock," said Zoron, "prepare the Time Transporter to send Aura back to Earth." Father Rock turned to Aura. "Aura, take this information down." Aura took out her Digimoid computer. "Ready," she replied.

Father Rock began dictating. "Go back to earth and pull up all the e-mails you have received from the TUW members on standby. The first order of business is that all the Team United Worldwide members come to the battle site. We need construction workers, engineers, site developers, carpenters, also computer technicians.

Have them set up a well camouflaged base camp in the woods near the mountain where the battle is to take place. Have team members with military, police, first aid and medical training come and assemble a medical facility at base camp. A first rate mental health medical facility is absolutely crucial during battle. We'll need the best minds in the business.

Team members with technological background will be assigned to a communication and command center. We need the most sophisticated computer equipment available. Aura, ask some of your trusted colleagues and students at the universities to bring equipment.

We need some real athletic types for the next teams to be assembled. Team One will consist of six motorcycle riders who can jump long distances on their motorcycles while carrying a twenty-pound backpack.

For Team Two, we will need four divers that can work down to 200 feet of depth and aren't afraid to dive at night. The night divers need metal detectors and light plants. Order ten thousand pounds of C4 compound and ten thousand feet of death cord.

Team Three will be a mountain climbing team of six that can rappel from high cliffs. Three of the climbers will need M79 grenade launchers. All climbers will need infrared glasses, plus walkie-talkies for the entire team. Two climbers will carry a small nuclear bomb device as a last-resort weapon.

Team Four shall include two long-distance bicycle riders, also three skateboard riders, jumpers, and slider style board riders. The skateboarders have some difficult maneuvers to make on the mountain side rocks, so recruit from extreme sports enthusiasts. Oh yes, two of the skaters must include a skydiver and sea diver.

One area we must penetrate requires a jump from a plane and the jumper must release his parachute upon landing and then put a skateboard under his feet as he lands on a rock slope that descends one thousand feet. At the bottom of the cliff the skateboard ride ends. The jumper flies off the cliff and dives one hundred and twenty-five feet into a lake.

A raft of equipment will await the Team diver. In the lake, he will place some explosive charges I have ordered throughout the battlefield." Aura said, "Okay, I got it, Father Rock." She read the information back to be sure she'd gotten everything.

Zoron said, "Set the Time Transporter and send Aura back to her studio on Earth." In moments, Aura appeared in her studio and started to broadcast e-mail to TUW members all over the world. Aura would order the Team United Worldwide to the battle site.

The Muzoids had disappeared. Zoron searched high and low, through all the caves and tunnels in the compound, but they could not be found anywhere. He confessed his growing concern to Dr. C. "Listen," said Dr. C. "I hear something." They heard a faint *tap, tap, tap*. "It seems to be coming from this direction." Father Rock pointed over a railing and down into the core of the time transporter energy device, sunken deep into the rock. Zap had entered a wrong code into his Digimoid and trapped all the Muzoids in a huge Plexiglas tube that was part of the conduit system. Zap's face was red with embarrassment. Zap put a note against the tube that said, "Dr. C, please enter this code into your Digimoid."

Dr. C burst out laughing, "Ha, ha, hee, hee. You little rascals! I should leave you there." All the Muzoids shook their heads and pleaded silently, "No, no, please no!" Zoron winked at Dr. C and Father Rock, saying, "Oh, let's leave them." They started walking away, leaving the Muzoids trapped in the tube. Their eyes got as big as silver dollars. Father Rock turned around, laughing, and said, "I got you back." Dr. C quickly punched in the proper code to release the Muzoids. The Muzoids winked out of the tube and back onto the landing pad. Spark ran and jumped in Dr. C's arms shivering. Dr. C said, "Why you were really scared. We would never leave you." Spark started laughing, as did Zon, Tink, and Electro. "We got you again." Father Rock said, "You darn Muzoids and your jokes." Dr. C said, "My word, you Muzoids are nuts."

Eighteen

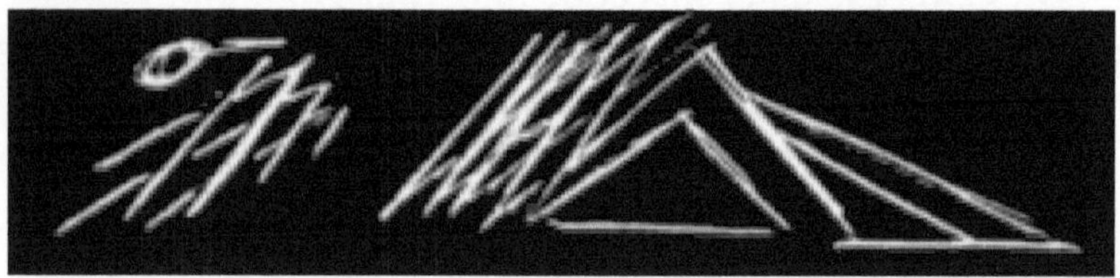

In no time, Aura received e-mails from all over the world confirming that the TUW members would meet where Aura had directed them to report. Things were shaping up fine. Aura left to set up a forward observation post in the woods near the battle site. She would be there to receive the Team as they arrived from all over the world.

The first to arrive was Frankie. Aura and Father Rock had hoped Frankie would be the operations manager for Team United Worldwide. He was trained in security, counter terrorism, and combat. He was a black belt in several martial arts. But Frankie's most appealing quality was his great compassion for humankind. He had dedicated his life to making the world a better and safer place to live. His moral integrity was unquestionable and he loved to work with young and old people.

Aura told Frankie of Father Rock's mission and the mission of Team United Worldwide. He immediately accepted the position of operations manager and agreed to add his talents to the Team to fight Demos and support Father Rock in his quest. Aura was pleased at Frankie's enthusiasm and progress in organizing the base camp. He quickly laid out the tactics and battle plans for the different teams. Aura reported the good news to Father Rock. Frankie had pledged himself one hundred percent to the Team.

Construction equipment arrived at the base camp. Frankie quickly set up the motor pool. Team members were dispersed all over the woods to set up camouflage outposts. The headquarters were assembled very quickly. Frankie reported, "Teams one, two, three and four have arrived and they have set up their tents and are settled in camp. They have been assigned to remote areas of the battle site to place different weapons before the battle begins."

Then the Muzoids appeared and got busy. Spark set off to sneak up the side of the mountain and hide nano chips. Spark had programmed these nano chips to be self-replicating robots. These robots would build traps and weapons as needed during the battle, and provide communication links to Goodtor, the Muzoid's 60 foot tall robot.

Goodtor had laser beams in his belt, eyes and forehead. He could become invisible. He could run fast and jump very high. His body could heat up to one thousand degrees or freeze to two hundred and sixty degrees below zero if necessary. If Demos won the battle, a built-in termination switch inside Goodtor would automatically obliterate the entire world and everything in it. Once Goodtor was in the termination mode nothing could stop him from blowing up. The team knew instinctively that if Demos ruled the world everyone would be better off dead. Life under his control would be unbearable.

Spark placed some Meltors, Electro hid some E-tors, Zap placed a giant Sleeptor cube and covered it up with camouflage, and Tink hid Freezon all over the battlefield. Zon divided himself in two parts. Fifty percent of his energy was in his own form, fifty percent of his energy was in the fractal state. He could become anything in the universe and become part of that mass of energy. So he became trees, rocks and would function as a forward observer to report back to Father Rock as Demos or the demons started approaching the area.

The D.T.s were set. The Muzoids would have to hit only one button on their Digimoid computer to activate their hidden destructive devices. Father Rock had ordered huge speakers be built into the rocks and mountain formation behind the stage. These huge speakers would project the music created by Father Rock and the Muzoids in battle.

The Muzoids placed a big screen that covered the ultrahigh frequency speakers. This was a special surprise gift from Father Rock to blast Demos away. Several pits were dug and filled with glue for Demos' Vibor demons to fall into. Frankie helped with the battlefield design. He told the Muzoids, "The strategy is to entice Demos to come after you. All you have to do is make him mad and he will send his Vibor demons in. Demos makes poor combat decisions when he gets mad, so can you make him mad?" "Okay, yeah, yeah, sure," Spark said, "We can make him mad."

Demos had planned his own surprise for Father Rock. The serpents, the Vibor demons and the flying demons had set a trap for the Muzoids. The demons hollowed out a big log and they slid inside the log. Then the demons dragged the log to the woods near Father Rock's base camp and hid it. Demos also made fake rocks. When the Muzoids stepped on the rocks they would fall inside and then the demons would eat them.

Demos had placed Eviltor the robot in a large cave. Demos chuckled evilly into his voice transmitter, "Now Father Rock, I have one of your robots. I have re-programmed him and named him Eviltor. One of his programs is called 'Kill Father Rock and the Muzoids'. Ha, ha, ha, ha. You know how powerful Eviltor is. By the way, Father Rock, give Aura a little hug and a kiss for me. Soon she will belong to me. Ha, ha, ha. Tell Aura I'm coming for her and she will be my bride." The demons laughed, sneered, and hissed. The cult chanted "Demos, Demos, Demos!"

FATHER ROCK

Father Rock was getting ready to time transport the large crystal to the stage when Demos' voice came out of nowhere, but he did not pause in his work. This crystal was ten feet by ten feet tall and cobalt blue, quite beautiful. The crystal must be placed exactly on stage at the perfect angles to redirect the laser beams from Father Rock's guitar. The battle would start at midnight. He had no time to pay attention to idle threats.

Frankie reported in. "We are combat ready. Teams one, two, three, four, five and six have completed their objectives. All devices are in place and prepared for initiation. We are combat ready. Everyone is on standby. In six hours the battle shall begin."

It was a very dark night, with no moonlight to speak of and very few stars. A cloud hung low between the two mountaintops. There was an eerie feeling in the air. Everything seemed too calm and dark. Demos was on one mountain, Father Rock on the other. The battle site was ready. Soon all kinds of trouble would break loose.

Nineteen

The power and intensity of the sound and laser power color forces to be used were not of this world, time or dimension. Father Rock knew Demos and the Vibors demons would use every evil trick in the book. Visual deception of double images was one of Demos' most powerful combat tactics. The entire mountain range was glowing with fields of wave energy.

Father Rock faced Demos across the valley. He began to glow as he pulled energy from the powers of the universe. His spiritual and dimensional powers were operating at their peak. Tink received a coded message from Father Rock. He took out his code book and read the secret message and said, "Okay guys, the skateboarders, Jibe and Smoker, are going to carry the gold crystals to put in the jet ski at the dock on the far side of the lake." Jibe said, "Smoker, there are two gold crystals. You carry one, I'll carry the other one. If either one of us gets hit the other must keep going and get the gold crystal to Captain Fisher. He'll be stationed on the lake using the crystal mounted on a jet ski as a mobile refractor for Father Rock's light beams."

As they jumped on their jet skateboards started down the side of a cliff, a flying Snake demon with two heads zoomed down at Jibe. Jibe pulled out his laser slingshot, put a red cube in it and fired it at the demon. The red cube hit the side of the mountain and exploded knocking a big hole in the side of the mountain. Smoker pulled out his slingshot, put a red crystal in it. He swung it over his head and let it go into the air.

The Snake demon spun right into the red crystal. *POW! BANG!* It was blown to pieces. Jibe said, "Good shot, Smoker, good shot." Jibe was looking at Smoker and didn't see a Vibor demon come out of the ground and shoot a low-frequency sound blast. *Wap!* Jibe was gone. Then the Vibor went after Smoker. He was right on his trail. Smoker would have to do some fancy riding. He jumped, flipped his board up in the air, did a triple flip over some large rocks. It was a long jump but he landed on his board. The Vibor demon took another shot at Smoker. It knocked a tree down. Smoker jumped in the air and rode the tree as it was falling to the ground. Then he jumped off the tree, landed on a flat rock at the edge of a cliff. He flew off the cliff and let his board fall. He pulled a ring on his parachute. It popped open and he glided over the lake, looking for Captain Fisher.

Spying the captain, Smoker pulled on the guidelines of his chute to adjust his direction, glided over him and dropped the tube with the gold crystal in it. The tube floated in the water. Mission accomplished. Captain Fisher picked up the tube and mounted it carefully on his jet ski. He took out his Digimoid computer and his secret code book and sent Father Rock the message: FISHER IN PLACE. GOOD LUCK TO ALL. KILL DEMOS.

The motorcycle riders had C4 compound on the back of their bikes. They had five miles of rough trail to ride past bloodthirsty demons. The C4 had to be placed on the other side of a cliff. It was a big jump over a

200-foot drop. The best riders in the world were recruited for this job. Blast and Tracer were the best and they thought they could make the jump although their chances seemed slim. They each had to carry 20 pounds of C4.

They were dressed all in black and on black bikes. "Ready to go," Blast said. Tracer gave Blast the old thumbs-up and they started down the trail. Blast held his hand up he spotted something up ahead. Blast got off the bike and walked about twenty feet. There he found a pit with sharp stakes pointing up. If Blast had not seen that they would be dead meat on a stake. Tracer said, "They must have this place wired and mined, we must be careful."

They rode around the pit, carefully scanning the ground for more traps. Soon a large serpent demon bird flew low over their heads. Blast thought, "*Now we got trouble, they know we are coming*". Blast and Tracer stopped for a closer look. Blast said, "I will go way out front. This way you can take off if you need to, no use both of us getting killed." Tracer said "no." Blast said, "I don't have a good feeling about this and Father Rock will need you with him if something happens to me. Take off for base camp and tell them what happened to me so they can change battle strategies." Tracer said "OK but I don't like it." Blast took off. He heard a sound like *Fezzz*. Blast looked around, he didn't see anything then again *Fezzz* and a small tap on his helmet. As Blast put his hand on his helmet, he felt something. He pulled it and there in his hand was a small dart. Luckily he had gloves on. "*Great*", he thought, "*poison dart demons. What next?*"

Blast devised a plan. *They probably think I have been hit. I will start riding crazy and they will think I am going down soon. No one survives the poison darts. Then I am going for the ride of my life. I will open this sucker up and won't stop till I am dead or jumping the cliff. ROAR!*, he let it all out at the max. It was all he could do to keep the bike up. Branches slapped at every part of his body. Blast made big jumps and slide as he flew down the trail and, wouldn't you know, Tracer was right on his back, flying like the wind. Two stars showing why they were champions.

Just ahead was the cliff. Full power all the way airborne, *zoom*! Blast and Tracer were laughing and screaming. A bomb went off near Blast and the explosion just missed him. Tracer was coming on strong then two explosions went off around him. Tracer zigzagged between the two explosions. “Got those moves from my football days,” he said laughing. Blast hit the high ride; fast and furious. Singing he flew through the air with the greatest of… Whoops! He was starting to fall. It looked as if he would be short on the jump and fall in the valley. “A little more just a little more, come on, come on. That’s it!” He barely made it. He screamed in victory, “Ya, all right.”

Tracer was right behind him. *Boom!* Tracer’s bike slammed down. He let out his famous rebel yell. “We made it, let’s get the C4 to the advance team.” Blast said “Good job.” Tracer said, “Good job? Why I think it was a terrific job. I just think we were wonderful. HA HA!” The two buddies rode away.

Twenty

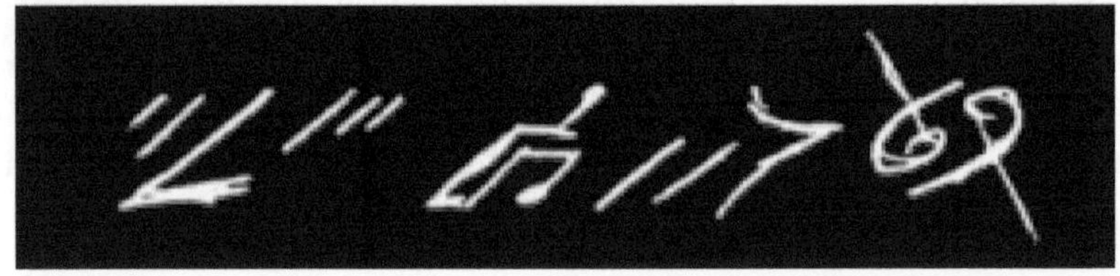

"Teams one, two, three and four have been sent forward," Frankie reported. Father Rock's large crystal was unveiled. Father Rock hit a note on his guitar and a laser beam shot a huge flash of different color lights and sound that illuminated and shook the entire mountain. A spectacular, dynamic visual barrage of red, green, blue and orange beams, rushed across the valley and hit Demos and his Vibors demons.

Demos was knocked down. He got up and pounded his keyboard, screaming furiously. Slobber flew from his lips and his eyes shot red balls of fire. Anger made his wiry black hair stand straight out from his head. The keyboard made a low-frequency sound so powerful it broke rocks on Father Rock's stage. Spark was slammed against the wall and knocked out. Now all the preparation and training would pay off. The Muzoids entered some codes into their Digimoids.

Spark woke up and said, "Okay guys, I'm ready. Let's get those

Vibors demons." Spark created a large ball of energy and propelled it into the center of a group of flying demons. *POW!* They exploded into a million pieces.

Meanwhile Electro was in a hot and heavy battle with Demos' band. Demos' band had three Vibor Demons playing drums. When they hit the drums a low death ray came from speakers mounted on the side of the mountain.

The battle was crazy and fierce: demons flying, bombs exploding. The entire mountain range was covered with dead demons. A flying demon crashed into the wall of speakers next to Father Rock and destroyed about 10 of the 100 big speakers. Father Rock just kept playing like a wild animal, blasting guitar sound at the speed of light. A deep hole opened by the stage about 50 feet from Father Rock and a Vibors demon shot up out of the ground firing a rocket launcher at Father Rock. It hit close to Father Rock, who yelled, "You want to play with me? How do you like this?" and he played a run on his laser guitar and a beam of white-hot energy fried the demon to a crisp. "Take that, you bunch of slimebags!"

Father Rock spun around and two more Vibors came at him. He breathed fire and one burnt demon was dead. "I am hot today!" he laughed. The other Vibor tried to sneak around the side of the stage. Father Rock hit his power button on his guitar, *BAM!* He blew the Vibors to pieces. The battle was raging now. Two of the Team members were trapped in a tree. They were trained snipers. The Vibors saw them and surrounded them. There must have been 20 demons around the tree, hissing and spitting poison. Some had already begun to wind their way up the trunk. There was no exit.

Spark saw the problem but could not help them. He had his hands full and he was pinned down. Spark took out his Digimoid and sent a message to Goodtor the robot. The giant robot appeared on the side of the mountain. He turned and shot a power ray *ZOOM!* He hit 5 of the Vibors. They returned fire at Goodtor. They hit Goodtor but he was not affected.

Goodtor put his huge hands in the air and rockets blasted out of each one of his fingers. *BAM! ZOOM!* Goodtor wiped them out. Spark hit his Digimoid and ordered Goodtor back to his post. Goodtor was to be saved to fight Eviltor, the evil robot. *BOOM! CRASH!* Explosions went off everywhere.

Tink saw where the bombs were coming from, a bunker on the north side of the battlefield, in a clump of trees. Tink worked his way over to the trees. There was a guard right in front of him. The guard came at Tink but Tink jumped in the air and shot a gas pellet. The gas knocked the guard out. Tink moved closer, he could see Serpent Demons and Vibors, about 25 or 30 of each kind of demon. It must be a command center, he thought.

Tink called for Electro and Zon on his Digimoid and told them to bring the cluster Jirow weapon. In about 20 minutes they arrived. "Well it's about time," Tink whispered. They set the weapon up. It could fire 500 rounds of small rockets every 10 seconds. What a war machine. Electro said "I want to do it." Zon said, "No. I want to do it." Tink said, "You two clowns. We are in a heated battle and you two want to argue over who will fire the J cluster. Well here is our anchor." Tink blasted away. "Man what firepower," Zon yelled. The Vibors and the Serpent Demons were falling. *RAT A TAT TAT*. "They are toast," Zon says, "You're making me hungry."

The Muzoids did their famous victory dance. Tink said, "Come on, you two, let's get back to it. Thinking about food at a time like this, really." The drums are next. "Electro," said Spark, "Let's get Demos' demons. Zon, back to your post." Electro pulled a tube of nano chips from his belt. He put some nano chips in his hand and jumped over the top of the demons, releasing the nanos over the ground where the demons were standing. The ground turned red hot. Electro yelled, "Hey boys, I'm going to teach you how to dance." As the ground got red hot the Vibors Demons jumped up and down holding their feet, yelling at Electro. Electro gave them a little musical victory dance.

Tink took his Digimoid computer and put in the code for Freezon, a D.T. that freezes everything it touches. Spark said, "Tink, freeze the drums." So Tink took a blue ball of Freezon and hit the drums. The drums froze. The demons were screaming, "ouch, ouch," jumping one foot to another. The drums start to melt on the hot ground. The Vibors Demons jumped on top of the frozen drums. "Ya, ah, ah," they said as they put their burnt feet in the ice. Tink said, "That will keep them busy for a while." All the Muzoids did a little victory dance, saying, "We are good, really, really good."

Demos saw what happened. He aimed his keyboard death ray at Tink and hit him with a low-frequency sound. Tink flew through the air and his head hit a tree. He was down, out cold. Zoron grabbed him by the belt and dragged him into the bushes, out of the line of fire. The Muzoids pulled out their laser wands that shoot different color rays. Spark took the red ray and hit Demos' keyboard. Smoke came from the keyboard.

Demos swung around and blasted Spark. He was out cold. Zap took his blue laser wand and hit Demos in the chest. Demos laughed, his red eyes glaring at Spark. Demos opened his robe and showed Spark he had a laser vest protector on. Demos said, "Spark, this is for you." His eyes shot a black beam. Spark and Tink had recovered from Demos' blast and were running around all over the place. Spark was fast, Demos' shot missed him.

Electro, Zap, Tink and Zon were dodging the demons' attack. Zon was hit with a poison dart from a demon. Electro pulled the dart out of Zon's leg and shot him with a serum that neutralized the Serpent Demon's poison. Vibor threw a Flying Demon in the air that went straight after Electro. Electro hit his Digimoid start button and shot an energy burst that fried the demon in midair.

Twenty-One

Aura and Frankie were viewing the battle from headquarters command center. Frankie said, “Aura, the Muzoids.” “Yes,” Aura said, “they are cute but fierce warriors.” “You got that right. They are fast and deadly in combat. And by the way, they can really dance. Ha, Ha,” Frankie said. He added, “We have killed 4251 demons and wounded 8452.” “How many Team members have we lost?” Aura said. Frankie answered, “2234 killed, 5645 wounded. What a terrible war this is, all the lost souls. The Muzoids have called hundreds of dimensional trancenders. Meltor, E-tor, Sleeptor, Freezon is all over the place."

Dr. C appeared at headquarters center. Aura and Frankie said, “Dr. C, you were supposed to stay on Galtor.” Dr. C said, “Hee, hee, hee. Well you know, I thought you might need me here.” Aura and Frankie said, “Okay,” as Dr. C passed by some magnetic land mine sweeping equipment. Frankie saw the needle go crazy. Frankie said, “Aura, could you come over here and look at this map?" Frankie pointed his finger at the dial counter. Aura raised her eyebrows. Frankie pulled his gun, and said, "All right, Dr. C or whoever you are, stand still."

Dr. C's eyes got five times larger than normal. In his eyes they could see demons of all types hissing and moaning, energy from the darkest side of the universe coming forward after Frankie and Aura. Frankie pulled his weapon and shot four times directly into the chest of the demon that disguised himself as Dr. C. These shots did not affect him. His huge eyes bulged horribly with the force of the demons trying to break free.

Aura grabbed a big blue crystal full of Freezon and threw it at the demon. The Freezon turned the demon into ice. Aura yelled, "Frankie, shoot it now! Shoot it now!" The demon shattered into a thousand pieces, closing the dimensional gateway.

Demos began summoning more of his demons. All at once Demos fired a massive sound charge. Father Rock was hit hard and it gave Demos the upper hand.

Father Rock repelled a vicious demon attack with a powerful force of high-frequency guitar sounds. Blasts of light flew from his fingertips as he played running his fingers up and down the neck of the guitar, he spun cosmic energy into a ball of universal force and flung it at the demons. Father Rock's multilevel dimensional attack of spears of sound and light force was so powerful that it overwhelmed Vibors demons. The Vibors became translucent and were forced into another time and dimension.

Twenty-Two

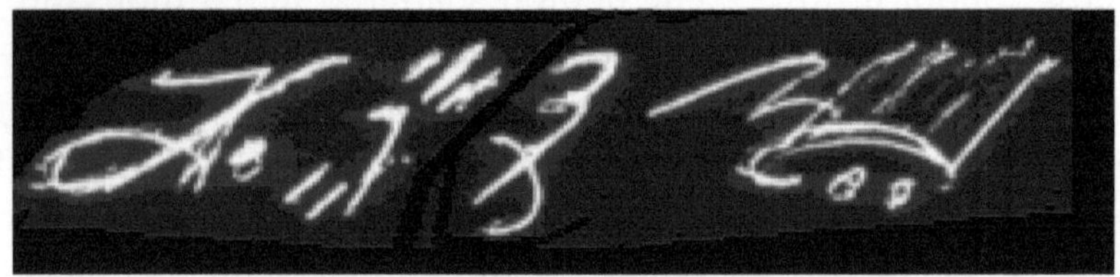

Demos activated Eviltor the robot. His sixty-foot body glowed and he emerged from the cave. Eviltor shot an energy beam that hit Father Rock. Father Rock was knocked to his knees. He knew that Demos' trick attack caught him off guard and he must recover fast. Father Rock pushed a button on his wristband and activated Goodtor.

Goodtor let loose with tremendous firepower. He fired a blast that struck Eviltor. Eviltor was rocked but did not go down. Both robots moved to the front of the stages. Father Rock and Demos moved to the side out of the way. Goodtor waited as did Eviltor. They just stood there looking at each other. Eviltor had a small red light flashing in his eyes and Goodtor had a white light flashing in his eyes. Everyone wondered anxiously what they were waiting for.

Then…*BAM*!…the earth shook. The two giants began an awesome battle. Goodtor opened up with a blast of rockets. *Zoom*! *Zoom*! Blazing hot trails of light streamed from the rockets as they shot at Eviltor. Eviltor countered the attack. *BAM*! *BAM*! He fired two large heat-guided missiles. So Goodtor fired two rockets just over the top of the missiles and the missiles followed the heat trail of the rockets. *BOOM*! *BOOM*! There was a white flash of light on a distant mountain top. When the smoke cleared the mountain was gone. Blown to smithereens. *ZAM*! The rockets hit all around Eviltor. *Bang!* One direct hit. Eviltor rocked back and forth, almost falling over.

A shield slid over Evitor's eyes and a black energy beam shot directly at Goodtor's eye shield. Goodtor opened his eye shield and a white-hot beam of energy shot out and hit the black energy in midair. The beams were halfway between the giant robots. As the beams collided fields of energy came from the two beams making a deep, heavy sound. The earth was shaking. Red, green, and bright yellow flashed all around the two beams. Spark said, "Wow! Hang on." Tink said, "Look, Eviltor is winning. His black energy is getting closer and closer to Goodtor." Zon said, "This doesn't look good." Father Rock was tapping a code in his Digimoid. Goodtor's silver metallic body turned red and his white energy beam got stronger as it moved closer and closer to Eviltor.

Demos said, "Rats, Goodtor is winning." Demos said, "Well it doesn't matter, Father Rock and I will settle the matter, once and for all, when I kill Father Rock. Then I will kill all those little weirdoes, the Muzoids." *BAM*! Eviltor's robot fell back into the cave on the left hand side of the stage.

The Muzoids got back in the action. The full battle raged. The Muzoids put up a great fight. They tapped their Digimoid computers and fought back against the Vibors Demons' attack. They bounced all over the stage. The Muzoids were ripping it up, great in battle. Spark tapped his Go key on the Digimoid computer and sent an order to Meltor. Demos tried to jam the transmission by pushing the button on his blocking device, but nothing happened to Spark's signal. Spark's transmission got through clearly. Demos said, "Jam, you fool, jam." Demos screamed at the top of his voice. Spark said to Tink, "Watch Meltor."

Meltors turned white, blue hot and generated ten thousand degrees of heat. Eviltor began to melt in seconds and was soon a pool of molten metal. The Muzoids rejoiced. "Yippee, yippee." Tink started doing the victory dance and Spark jumped in his little legs moving very fast. He was yelling, "Got you, dirt bag." Zon did a spinning dance, spinning round and round "WHOPEEE! Eviltor is burnt out, Ha Ha, for good." Electro did a little jig and played a Muzoid bagpipes while singing, "Eviltor is no more, that is for sure. He is one dead robot and that is that."

Father Rock was in a daze from a direct hit. He was propped on one knee using his guitar as a crutch. He activated the life cycle energy pulse transmitted through the dimensional chamber from the top of the crystal in his guitar. Laser beams filled the mountain with bright multicolors of energy: red, purple, green, violet and blue. Father Rock was quickly energized. He jumped to his feet with a scream and played super speed runs on his guitar, the most awesome sounds ever played. Father Rock played faster and faster. His clothes looked like sparkling diamonds. He seemed to move in slow motion as his energy intensified. His entire body reflected every color in the universe. In opposition, Demos played his keyboard, making eerie, weird sounds. Low-frequency booming sounds, but Demos was no match for Father Rock.

Demos turned into purple energy and hit the death ray on his keyboard. Father Rock deflected the death ray with his guitar. Father Rock's entire body was now energized with blue-white energy. His white hair was blowing in the wind. Red, green, purple, blue and violet colors flashed up and down his body. Father Rock shot two laser beams from his eyes. Electricity shot from his third eye, then Father Rock held his hand in the air and threw a ball of fire. Father Rock screamed like a wild animal, firing shot after shot from his mouth, while playing lightning fast runs on his guitar. His hands looked like a blur of white energy. The sound and light energy were amazing, beyond furious, beyond description in dynamic splendor and in awesome bewilderment.

Demos was consumed with anger. He was pounding on his keyboard death ray. His purple robe had turned jet black. Lightning shot from Father Rock's eyes and hit Demos in the leg. Demos screamed in agony. Electric sparks jumped up and down his black and purple robe and his fingernails were making a clicking sound.

Father Rock looked at his arm; it was bleeding. He placed his hand on the wound and it stopped the bleeding and was healed. *ZAM!*. Demos used his Vibor ray and projected two Vibor Demons on stage to attack Father Rock. One was a big green serpent-like demon with large fangs. Its eyes looked like two slits filled with black moving creatures, surely the doorway to madness. The Serpent demon coiled, lashed out and wrapped itself around Father Rock. It bit him on the leg and blood poured from the wound. Spark saw that Father Rock was in big trouble. The second demon bit Father Rock's other leg.

Demos laughed madly, a crazed look in his eyes. "Now who is the greatest ruler in the universe? It's me. It's me." He screamed, and his low gravelly voice echoed through the valley. Spark had to move quickly. He jumped on stage and took out a tube of Nano chips programmed to destroy any living organism they touched. Spark jumped on the Serpent Demon's back. "One drop of the Nano and you're dead." He was worried he might kill Father Rock with this move, but he had no choice. Just as he was pouring the Nano the second serpent slipped up behind Spark and bit him. The pain was intense. Spark did not flinch. Father Rock said, "Spark, save yourself." Spark did not listen. He poured the first drop on the Serpent Demon, and it made a hissing sound and dropped dead. Spark got a drop on the second demon and it too died. Spark was in bad shape and so was Father Rock. Spark looked at Father Rock crying, "OH OH," as tears ran down his face, "Father Rock, the pain is so bad."

Father Rock laid his hands on Spark and healed him. Spark smiled and thanked him, but Father Rock shook his head, "You are so brave and a good friend. It is I who should thank you, Spark."

Father Rock then placed his hands on his own wounds. He closed his eyes and bowed his head and his wounds were healed. Demos screamed, "I will destroy you!" Father Rock answered, "Demos, you cannot destroy me. I have all dimensional and spiritual positive forces of the universe. All that is good is mine. All that is evil is yours. I will destroy all evil from now until eternity." Father Rock shot white-hot energy from his eyes and mouth. "The universe belongs to the power of good forces." Father Rock struck a tremendous, thunderous burst of sound and white energy and hit directly into Demos' third eye.

Father Rock said, "I am the sword. I severed your evil energy, Demos." Demos screamed and fell lifeless on the mountainside. Without their leader, the last of the demons were quickly dispatched by the Muzoids to another dimension. The Muzoids started their victory dance again, jumping and yelling. Dr. C even joined in. "Ha, hee hee hee, We showed them, yes, we did indeed." Frankie and the Team members celebrated wildly.

"Guess what everyone?" Father Rock said, "My Aura and Zoron are to be wed." Everybody screamed, "Yes, yahoo!" Father Rock said, "We are going to have the biggest wedding ever held. Father Rock then mind projected the announcement to all things that exist. A white flash came from his hand and he said, "I have just invited millions of guests."

Zoron and Aura kissed, overjoyed that they were getting married. Father Rock would give Aura away at the wedding ceremony to be held in the Celestial Garden, famous for its large collection of statues and fountains that Father Rock had designed. Giant light pink and blue swans swam in a magnificent large lake surrounded by wildlife of all kinds. The animals and plants were gifts to Father Rock from other worlds and dimensions. In the center of the lake was a white and gold fountain. The fountain was twenty stories tall, the water deep blue and pure sweet to drink and soft to touch. The fountain shot water 250 feet into the air. It was rich and vibrant and dreamlike in the Celestial Gardens. No one could ever forget its colorful sights and the splendor of its presence. Dr. C would perform the wedding ceremony and the Muzoids would be the best men. The wedding would be broadcast to TUW members everywhere.

Twenty-Three

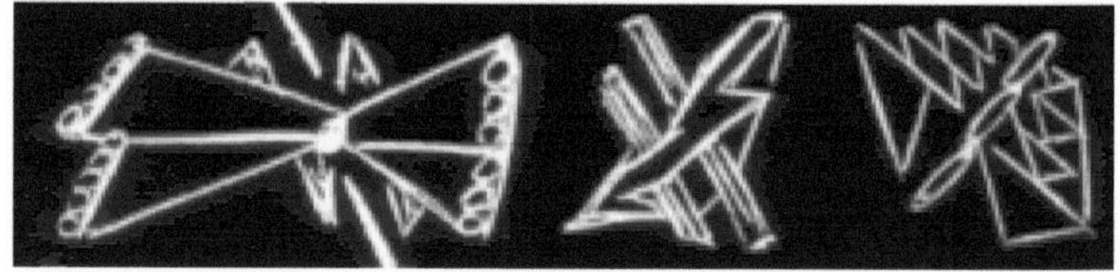

Time passed quickly as everyone prepared for the wedding. *The big event was finally here.* The Muzoids cooked for three days. The Muzoids were the best cooks in the universe. All of the people worked very hard to put the wedding together. The wedding began with recordings of Father Rock playing very spacey soft music, angelic music. The setting was beautiful. Trees with golden leaves made chime sounds as the soft breeze blew them into one another. White, light blues and gold were the wedding colors. Gems were inlaid into angelic statues that gave off the light of love and energy, and dominating the scene, the Tree of Life stood green and majestic. It was like a dream. At the same time it was so intense guests felt chills as Aura and Zoron appeared on a gold flying disc and gently landed.

Zoron took Aura's arm. He was regally dressed in a white robe trimmed with gold. The guests oohed and aahed as they passed by, floating on a white cloud to the podium. Little silver and gold specks sparkled in the air. A fragrant smell of roses permeated the garden. Everyone felt the magical energy of their love. Aura was a breathtaking bride, her delicate gold lace veil wafting on the gentle breeze, her white dress iridescent in the evening sun. Happiness radiated from her center and spread throughout the garden.

The day was perfect. The Celestial Garden was filled with lots of flowers in every color in the spectrum. The sky was streaked with white, purple, pink, red, bright yellow and the clouds were puffy and soft. They filled the sky. Everything was perfect, like a master artist's greatest painting. The sweet sounds of Father Rock's music created a euphoric karma, a light spiritual glow to the atmosphere. A majestic state of tranquility was present. White doves flew overhead. The Muzoids were overjoyed, dancing, crying and laughing at the same time. Everything was in pastel colors, an unearthly pastel world of color energies. Millions of guests were there from all the dimensions as Dr. C began the ceremony of eternal love.

Aura was beautiful, dressed in a long wedding robe trimmed in gold sparks that glistened with the diamonds woven into the fabric. Aura's long blond hair shimmered in the sunlight like a million stars. Her deep blue eyes twinkled in the sunlight. She smiled with the happiness of love in her heart.

Zoron stood tall and handsome in his white robe of gold specks lined with gems, cut from the same cloth as Aura's robe.

Dr. C wore his black formal attire of spiritual universal oneness. He began the ceremony, "There has never been a wedding this big and beautiful in all the dimensions. This is a very special event. All is tranquil, all is peaceful and the light of love is shining brightly on Aura and Zoron. If you wish to be as one…in love…in life forever, hold your hands together." Aura and Zoron turned and faced one another. "Now join your hands above your heads." At that instant, Aura's body radiated pink energy and surrounded Zoron. Zoron's body became blue energy and surrounded Aura. The two lovers were joined in the light of eternal love.

Flashes of light red, green, purple, yellow, violet and orange formed one constant white energy force around Aura and Zoron.

Father Rock proclaimed, "They are as one, from Earth to infinity." Father Rock was overjoyed. He picked up his special guitar of white and blue crystal and began to play beautiful, cosmos unified dimensional music. As Father Rock played, a vision came out of the white energy. The physical shadows of Aura and Zoron's images became stronger and stronger. Then they appeared in full image. They held up their hands. The guests clapped and cheered. The Muzoids laughed with joy.

The sounds Father Rock played brought the spirits of all love and positive energy together. Father Rock closed his eyes. He was in a spiritual trance, slowly rocking back and forth as he played. Father Rock was the All. In the light of oneness, with the all of the all, of everything that was and would ever exist.

Then as far as one could see, craft from all the dimensions appeared. Father Rock's music filled the universe with inspirational love and joy as he played. Father Rock's hair and robe lit up with energy and the sounds he played were rich and sweet and full of life. Father Rock projected a powerful light force of red, purple, green, blue-violet and blue colors. As the spectrum changed colors, the spacecraft changed in time. The feeling of love, light and peace was awesome.

Everyone in attendance wore a unicrystal necklace and ring. As Father Rock played, the unicrystal necklaces and rings shot out a spectrum of colors. The matching pattern of lights and energies created by all of the sources of light became one united frequency. Now finally, all seemed to be at peace. They stood in the light of love as one united family from Earth to infinity…

Then There Could Be Seen The Terrible Demos

... lying on the sacrificial table, dead. His hand, his black nails, his wrinkled hand, his frozen hand appears lifeless yet, incredibly, Demos' hand moves and the universe trembles knowing that Demos is not dead.

The End of the Beginning

TERRY BROOKS

As I cross the last “T” and dot the last “I” of Father Rock on Friday the 13th, August 2004, the thunder roars and the lightning flashes. The world seems to cry tears tonight with the heavy down pour of rain and the wind blowing at 105 mph, tearing my large white wooden gate from its’ post bending the hinges into a cork screw shape. Winds pound my home, at times shaking the walls and rattling the windows, creating a loud eerie howling sound, as I work by candle light in my study, I cannot help but feel sadness that all is left is to sign my name to the Father Rock book, a labor of love.

Until next time
Stand in the light of love
T. R. BROOKS

FATHER ROCK

Twenty-Four

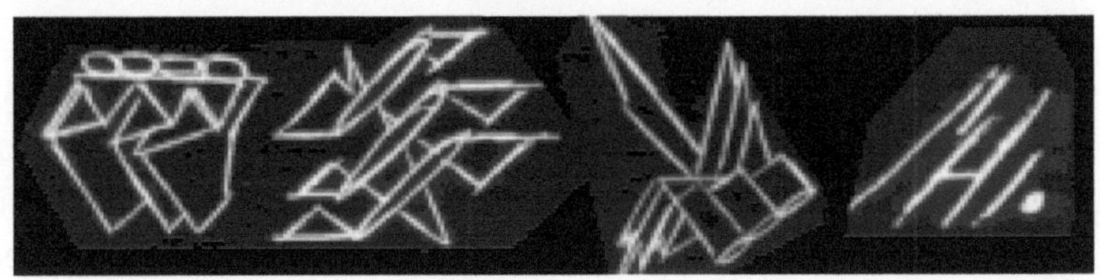

"I cannot believe it's been 15 years since the war with Demos." Aura commented as they waited for the time portal. *A flash of purple light came, and then white light illuminated what looked like a tunnel.* Aura, Zoron and Toron, their ten-year-old son, prepared themselves for the trip to Galtor. Toron's eyes were wide with excitement. "Dad, Tell me about the great war between my Grandfather, Father Rock and Demos." "Ok," Zoron said for the thousandth time, "I will tell you the story again."

At the same time a black energy capsule radiated in space on an invisible plane called Sintor. As far as everyone knew Demos was dead, but in reality, he awaited in a black energy field within Sintor, gathering strength for the next battle. Soon, he would be ready to take over a new human body. Once in this human form, he was determined to kill Father Rock once and for all.

Zoron began, "Father Rock faced a big battle, huge in magnitude. First, he called in his team of leaders: Dr. C, Aura, myself, the Muzoids. Then he called in Frankie and the TUW (Team United Worldwide) to fight Demos and his demons. The battle took place on a mountain range. The winner of the battle would change the future of all existing things. Father Rock was for all that was good. Demos and his demons were for all the evil forces of the universe."

Toron said, "Go on, go on!" "Well the battle was amazing. This was a fierce battle. There was lots of heavy combat. The lights from Father Rock's guitar lit up the mountain range. Red, blue, green and purple lights flooded the sky. Father Rock shot beams of energy and fire from his eyes and mouth. He threw balls of white-hot energy. His long white hair flowed like wild strains of electricity. His hair and robe changed colors as he played lightning fast. He played screaming runs up and down the neck of his guitar. The Muzoids used the Dimensional Transcenders of all kinds wielding awesome powers. Father Rock said, "I have transcended time and space to the now of your existence. I am Father Rock. I am the carrier of the light to destroy Demos and his demons."

"What happened to the Muzoids?" asked Toron. Zoron said, "They have lived very well since the battle." Toron asked, "Where do they live? Can I see them?" "Oh no," Zoron said. "The Muzoids are great warriors. They are only called in extreme times of crisis. They live in the Muzoid dimension. Now they have children like we have you. They are very happy with their families. They enjoy a full and peaceful life."

Demos looked in his magic viewer. *Yes, that's right, tell the little brat about how you and the Muzoids helped Father Rock kill me. I have new demons now, more powerful than before and my energy is stronger than ever. I have only one problem, the invisible planet Sinton. I cannot break the energy field surrounding it. Someone must pass through the Sinton energy field. Then I can transcend my black energy into their body and take over their soul. Then I shall kill all of you, but I will kill Father*

Rock last so he can suffer seeing all his team and family die before his eyes. Ha Ha Ha. I shall be the ruler of all that is.

Zoron said, “Demos was a terrible and wicked demon of the dark forces. We are all glad he is dead.” Toron was full of questions, as always. “Dad, how old is grandfather?” “They say he has always been and he shall always be, he is the infinite one. He is timeless. He is the carrier of the light.” *Flash, flash white lights slowing them to a stop.* “We are here,” said Toron, “I can’t wait to see grandfather.” *A field of energy melted in front of them.* Father Rock was standing on a new device he had invented. It was a buster beam that allowed consciousness in multi-dimensions at one time. and also allowed in-depth functions in each dimension with trillions of tasks working simultaneously.

Father Rock saw the group. “Hello, come in, everyone.” His voice was filled with cheer. “Give me a big hug. I have a surprise for you. We have a visitor.” Toron said, “Who is it?,” jumping around with excitement. Father Rock said “It’s Dr. C.”

Dr. C came through an energy field, dressed all in black with an Irish beret on his head, snake cane in hand, and puffing on his crooked pipe saying in his Irish brogue, “Ho ho, hee hee, it’s me, Dr. C.” “Gee,” Toron said, “I know who you are! You helped grandpa kill Demos." “Right you are. Guilty again. This is true.” Dr. C reached his hand to Toron’s ear. “What’s this Toron? Got it, hold on. Well, will you look at this!”

Toron’s eyes popped wide open. “What? Let me see.” “It is yours,” Dr. C said, placing a shining red and blue crystal in Toron’s hand. “It has magic powers. If you ever need the power of the crystal, hold it to your forehead.”

Toron said, “Wow!” Father Rock walked up to Toron and put his hand next to his other ear. He said, “This blue and red crystal has all powers of the universe. It is hidden in the unicrystal.”

“Oh boy, I have always wanted my own unicrystal necklace and now I have one." Toron held up the sparkling crystal for his parents to see.

Father Rock said, "You shall be the one to carry on our beliefs of universal peace, love, light and harmony to the future generations."

Father Rock's eyes glazed as he experienced a flashback. *An image of Demos appeared in a dark place, his evil eyes aglow. Demos made a growling sound.* He shook his head to clear it. Zoron asked, "Father Rock what's wrong?"

"Oh it's ok, just bad memories from the past." Father Rock picked up his laser guitar, a new model and played a blazing run of wild sounds. Toron jumped up and down. It was the first time he'd seen his great-grandfather play. Color lights flashed. Toron said, "Gee, that's great", as blue, red, and green beams shot all over the place from Father Rock's guitar. His fingers were a blur as they ran up and down the neck of the guitar. The sounds were ripping wild, awesome. His long white hair danced in the wind and changed colors: purple, red and blue. His whole body was energized. As Father Rock spun around shooting lightning bolts from his eyes and fire from his mouth, Toron screamed. "Yes! Yes! Grandpa!" "He can make that guitar scream. He's a cosmic rock star!" Dr. C said, "That he can. young lad. Ho Ho, Hee Hee, Father Rock always has some musical magic up his sleeve."

Father Rock finished his performance with a wild riff as everyone clapped and yelled. Then his mood turned serious. "Zoron, I heard about a new crystal. It's the Claybous crystal. It's a mixture of several of the tenth-power crystals. One problem, it's located in a very dangerous part of the universe."

Zoron asked, "Do you need this crystal?" Father Rock shook his head. "No, it's too far and too dangerous to go after. It's in the Remon sector. But it is good information to have, just in case."

Zoron shuddered. "Oh, no, not the Remons." "Yes," Father Rock said, "as you know the Remons absorb all energy they touch. They are the cannibals of the universe."

Another flashback transfixed Father Rock. He saw Demos' image with his red eyes aglow. “Zoron, come with me. Get Dr. C. We must have an emergency meeting,” said Father Rock. They went into a safe green energy field room that repels all outside sound and energy. “Twice today I have had flashbacks of Demos.” Zoron and Dr. C gasped. Father Rock continued, “Don’t alarm Aura or Toron. I am asking now, are you sure Demos is dead?”

“Yes of course.” Zoron answered. “We saw the body; it was scorched almost beyond recognition.”

“Ok,” Father Rock said, “I have a mission for the two of you. Transport yourself back to earth. Go to the sacrificial altar and make sure Demos’ body is still there. I’ll keep Aura and Toron busy while you are gone.”

Twenty-Five

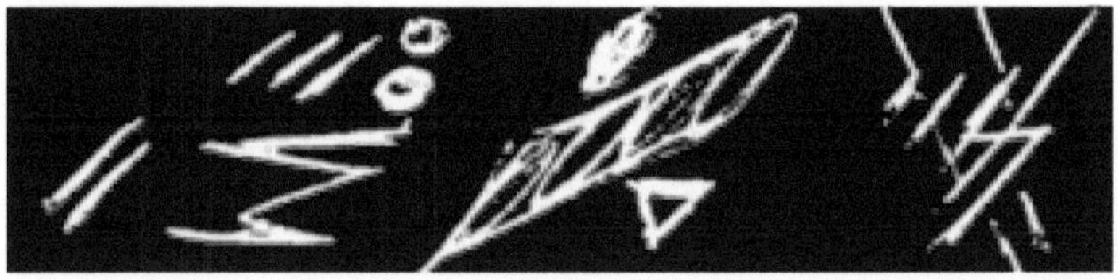

Back on Earth, Dr. C and Zoron went to the sacrificial altar. The charred body lay there cold and lifeless, just as they'd seen it last. Both men got chills as they looked at the evil Demos' body. Dr. C said, "I had forgotten how evil he was. It gives me the creeps just looking at him."

"Yes, he was very bad, an evil monster. I am sure glad he is dead," Zoron said. "Let's report back to Father Rock that Demos is dead."

They transported back to Galtor. Aura, Toron and Father Rock were having a ball playing around, joking and laughing. They had prepared a big meal. "Welcome back!" called Aura. "We fixed your favorite meal, turkey with all the trimmings."

"Right you are," smiled Dr. C.

Father Rock whispered, "What about the body? Was it still there?" Dr. C said, "It's there." Father Rock sighed with relief. "I must be having bad memories, that's all."

FATHER ROCK

Zoron said, "While we were on earth, we stopped to see Nerdboy Baxter."

"Ah… is he over the XX49 being replaced with an olive?" Aura chuckled at the memory of Baxter's tantrum.

"That was such a long time ago. How is he?" Father Rock said. "Is he still at NASA?" "Oh yes. They give him anything he wants, but all he wants is a project, pizza and his computer and he is happy. He asked about you…and about Aura, of course." Zoron winked at his wife.

"Baxter told us that a launch mission is scheduled soon and he hopes you will come to see it and meet a new young astronaut. His name is Zander."

Father Rock said, "Of course I will. I will give him a unicrystal necklace."

Two months later at NASA, Father Rock, Aura and Toron met Dr. C at the launch site. He said, "I have a surprise for you. Zander is my grandson. Ah, here he comes now. A strapping Irish lad, tall, with red hair and blue eyes. Good-looking chap, don't you think?" Dr. C glowed with pride. "Yes," said Father Rock, "very much so."

Zander greeted Doctor C with a big hug. "Hi, Grandpa!" He extended a warm handshake to Father Rock. "Hello, sir. Thanks for coming. I have always wanted to meet you. Grandpa told me so much about you," Zander said.

Father Rock answered truthfully, "It's my pleasure." He introduced the rest of the party. "Zander, this is my grand-daughter, Aura, her husband, Zoron, and their son, Toron, is my great-grandson."

"Gee, could I be an astronaut some day?" asked Toron.

Zander nodded. "You can be anything you want to be. You just have to work hard and stay focused. Oh, look, here comes Baxter." They heard him muttering as he hurried towards them. "Oh my, oh me."

"What's wrong, Baxter?" Zander grabbed his arm to get his attention.

Toron whispered to his dad, "What's that red stuff all over his shirt?" Zoron snorted. "Pizza. He loves to eat pizza. I've never seen him without sauce."

Baxter was breathless from his rush across the grounds. "Well you see, they think I am wrong, but I believe the new directional controls have a flaw in their design. This would put the StarFlyer off its trajectory about one half of one millionth of a degree. I have told Doctor Stanley, but with his big ego, he can't ever admit to a mistake. His stupid ego could put the whole project and Zander's life in jeopardy."

Zoron said, "Are you sure?"

Baxter shrugged, "I extrapolated the figures five times. I know I am right."

Baxter, although he was upset, saw a chance to get even with Zoron for taking his XX49 power buster and placing a black olive in its place. Zoron had an equipment pack marked Top Secret. While Zoron and the others whispered, Baxter unzipped and lifted the top of the pack, then he poured Super Glue all over Zoron's equipment. Then he placed a note inside the pack on top of the equipment. "Remember the olive. Ha ha. Baxter got you back." He put the top back down and zipped the equipment pack, laughing under his breath.

Zoron said, "Baxter, you should try again. Go over the math one more time." Baxter said, "It's too late. The countdown horn is sounding." Zander said, "That's my signal to report to the shuttle. Don't worry, Baxter, everything will be all right." Everyone gave him the thumbs-up. Zander hugged Dr. C again. "See you soon, Grandpa, I love you." He climbed into the jeep, his ride to the StarFlyer. It was one hour till final countdown.

The hour passed quickly and then it was time…10-9-8-7-6-5-4-3-2-1 liftoff!. The ground rumbled as the StarFlyer took off. They all watched the StarFlyer sail through the clear blue skies of Florida.

Father Rock said, "Baxter, try your extrapolations by putting in the one-half of one-millionth degree and give me a true projection for the StarFlyer." Baxter whipped out his portable computer and tapped away.

FATHER ROCK

After twenty-five minutes Baxter said, "I got it. Here is the information you wanted." Father Rock said, "Thank you Baxter. We must get back to Galtor."

Back at home, Father Rock went straight to his Digimoid master computer and fed Baxter's calculations into the universal galactic map locator. The computer printed out a chart. "Here we go," said, Father Rock. "Ok. We go to the Startron sector force region then to Sintor and on to Bright Star galaxy. Nothing there. It looks okay. Father Rock said to himself, *I must stop worrying about things so much.*

Suddenly, he was transfixed by a vision. Demos was shooting his death ray at him. Father Rock returned fire, a laser blast at Demos. *Wap*! It hit Demos. Demos screamed, "I'll kill you." *Zap*!

"Father Rock," Zoron was asking loudly, "hellooo? how does the trajectory look?"

"What? Oh yeah, it looks fine. No dangerous areas in Zander's path. The StarFlyer will be fine. The new trajectory still leaves enough fuel for the return trip, so no problems there, and there are no obstacles in its path."

Far away, Demos looked in his viewer. "Ah ha, look at this. The space shot puts the StarFlyer on a trajectory directly through Sintor."

Twenty-Six

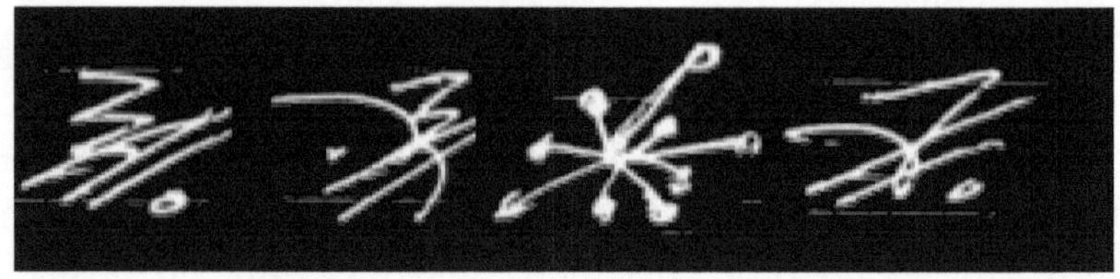

"Ha Ha!" Demos roared in his deep, gravelly voice. "So Zander is coming to give me his body. How perfect. I shall be free to rule the darkness. Once again the power of darkness shall prevail." Demos laughed wickedly.

"NASA Command Center to Zander. All systems are go." Zander replied, "Roger. All systems are go, over and out." The StarFlyer rushed toward Demos' home. Three days after the ship approached Sintor, Zander sent a report to NASA. He felt a vibration. He was dizzy as he looked at the gauges. There was no indication of vibration showing. All at once a black energy invaded the StarFlyer. Zander tried to avoid it but there was no where to hide. A black ball of energy formed about a foot in front of his face. The black energy focused to a one-inch beam. The beam slowly moved to a point in the center of Zander's forehead. *Zap*! The black beam shot right into his third eye. Zander trembled; his veins turned black. His skin turned red, then a green yellow. He shook and sweated a black liquid. His fists clinched and he fell back in his chair, totally exhausted. About three hours passed before Demos awoke in Zander‘s body. He felt rested and strong. He gave the Command Center, a yes Check; systems are go, over and out. In 21 days the StarFlyer would be on earth. Demos thought to himself, I will return as an astronaut…a hero. His evil laugh echoed as he beamed in delight.

21 days passed and the StarFlyer landed at NASA. A crowd of people cheered Zander as he came down the walkway. Demos looked at the big crowd through Zander's eyes. *Look at this, the fools are even cheering me. You idiots, you're all mine to do my bidding. Ha Ha, I shall rule everything that exists. You will all be my slaves.*

Zander walked into the Recovery Center at NASA. “Take me to the Code Center,” he demanded.

The officer in charge said, “Sir, you know the rules. No one is allowed in the Code Room, not even you.” The officer looked into Zander's eyes and two red dots appeared that put the officer under Zander's control. Helpless to resist, he entered his secret code in the keypad. Demos ordered the officer to sit in a chair near the door while he memorized the secret codes he needed. When he finished, he walked to the officer and ordered him to stand. They walked out of the Code Room. Demos released his hold on the officer. Zander looked at the officer and said, “You're right, no one in the Code Room. I was just testing you.” The officer didn't remember a thing. Demos thought, *I must set up my new home.*

Zoron and Father Rock approached the Recovery Center. They planned to congratulate Zander and head for home so he could get some rest. As they walked toward him, Father Rock could see a black aura around Zander's body, glowing darkly in the fluorescent light. Father Rock thought perhaps he had picked up some negative energy charge on reentry and that the negative energy charge would dissipate in a few days.

But as Father Rock touched Zander’s hand, he felt something far more powerful and evil. “Something wrong, Father Rock?” Zander's eyes widened innocently as he searched Father Rock's face. Father Rock said, “Not really, we are going home. We wanted to congratulate you on your mission. We shall be leaving now.”

Zander said mockingly, “Have a safe trip.” They parted. *Wish I could have killed Father Rock right then*, thought Demos as they walked away. *That’s right, the bunch of you, run home, I’ll get you all soon enough.*

Twenty-Seven

Father Rock, Aura, Zoron, Toron and Dr. C were glad to be back on Galtor. Father Rock said, “Dr. C, something is wrong with Zander.” Father Rock put his hands over his eyes to see his one-cycle energy force, a red dot of energy that leaves his body through his third eye every three seconds with another red energy returning to his third eye every one and one half seconds. Father Rock could see a red energy. This energy looked like a cell that floats gently in outer space. Sometimes it was purple depending upon our universe’s location, but always the same time factor no matter what outside forces and energies came in contact with the one-cycle energy force. Father Rock removed his hands from his eyes and said, ”The harmonious frequencies of all existing things are as one. There are no dominant discords. Still, I have seen a black energy field around Zander.”

Dr. C said, “Oh no! Demos? But how could that be? Demos is dead.

We saw the body."

Father Rock nodded. "I can think of only one explanation. Demos could have projected his black energy from his body just before it died."

"Perhaps." said Dr. C. "Shall I give Zander a visit?"

"Yes, but if Demos has taken Zander's body as his energy capsule you can't let him suspect you are on to him. Demos will kill you on the spot."

Dr. C said, "I'll be careful. Zander is my grandson. I must know the truth."

"There is only one way to test Demos' black energy." Father Rock held up a handful of small green crystals. "These crystals respond to dark energy. In Demos' presence they will turn black. Be very careful."

Dr. C decided to make it look like a plausible accident when he encountered Zander, so he made an appointment to meet with Nerdboy Baxter. As Dr. C neared the lab, he saw Zander walking towards the astronauts' training center. Zoron had placed the green crystals in the eyes of the snake head carved on his walking stick. Dr. C only needed to be in his presence for two minutes. Zander turned his head and walked faster, trying to avoid Dr. C.

Dr. C yelled, "Zander, over here." Demos thought, oh no, what does he want?

"Over here," Dr. C yelled again, waving his snake cane in the air. Dr. C said, "Zander, I'm so glad I ran into you! I didn't get a chance to congratulate you on your mission."

"Ok, now you have." Zander said, "Thanks. I've got to go." Demos knew that he could not fool Zander's grandfather for long.

Dr. C thought fast. He needed two minutes! "Wait, there's something I've been meaning to discuss with you. Do you feel that the vibratory frequencies of all existing things can be divided by the number of oscillations of the out band frequencies calculated as the one sum total of the universe?"

Demos said, "Well Doc, that's your problem. I am not a quantum physicist professor. I must go."

"Right," Dr. C said, "I just thought you might be interested, given the studies we used to do together. Well, then, how was your trip? Got your earthlegs back yet? Any lingering sickness or aches and pains from zero-G?"

Exasperated, Demos barked, "No, I'm fine, and…I'm late to an appointment with the chief, so I have to go right now. Goodbye, Doc."

Off you go, then, cheerio." Dr. C let Zander get out of sight before looking at his cane. It came as no surprise to Dr. C that the eyes of the snake were black. Zander's behavior could not have been stranger given their warm relationship. "Doc" indeed! Dr. C. thought, *Oh no, Demos is alive. He's back to do his evil deeds again.*

Dr. C went right back to tell Father Rock the bad news. He held his cane in the air so Father Rock could see the black eyes. "Just as I suspected, Demos cast his black energy into space and Zander passed through a negative energy field. Demos and his demons are still alive. We must prepare for battle. Get Zoron and Aura in here. I will ask the Muzoids to come here to put the battle strategies together." He tapped a code in his Digimoid computer.

They came at once, Spark, Tink, Zap, Electro, Zon bouncing all over the place. Tink bounced over to Dr. C and said, "What's up Doc?" Before Dr. C could answer, Tink gave him a big kiss on his bald head. Dr. C said "They're crazier than ever." Zap slipped up behind Zoron and pinched him on the arm. Zoron said, "You little rascal, I knew it was you." Electro flew over in Aura's arms and gave Aura about ten quick kisses and said, "I love you Aura." Aura blushed and said, "I love you, too, Electro." Spark headed right for Father Rock and sat on his shoulder. Blinking his eyes he said, "You called? Our magic is at your command." Toron was delighted to meet the Muzoids he'd heard so much about.

"Everyone, I have bad news. Demos is alive." Father Rock told them the whole story. "Fortunately, Demos thinks we still believe he is dead so we have the upper hand at this time. Zoron, I need the Claybous crystal. As you know it's in the Remon sector."

Aura said, "Not the Remons."

Zoron took her hand and said, "Don't worry, it'll be ok." Aura's eyes filled with tears. The Muzoids were very quiet and serious, remembering how terrible the battles were with Demos. "We must upgrade the Digimoid computers immediately." They moved to a corner table to begin programming.

"Dr. C," Father Rock said, "I need some research on Remons. Try to find their weakness. How can we block their ability to absorb energy?"

"Righto, I am on it," said Dr. C.

"Aura, get in touch with Team United Worldwide. We must put a team together. The last battle never really ended because Demos still lives. The battlefield shall be earth again in the mountains."

Twenty-Eight

Zoron prepared to travel to Remon. The first step would be the most difficult. Dr. C's research pointed to a sole, horrifying conclusion. He could only pass the powerful Remon energy cannibals if he were dead. Zoron's body could not have any sign of life energy. His heart must be stopped and he must be put in suspended animation for three days. The computer would resuscitate him once the ship was beyond the Remon's energy field. Once on Remon, there were other challenges. Every four days, Remon was deluged by acid that fell like rain. Zoron had only four days to retrieve the crystal and leave the planet or the acid would dissolve him and his ship.

The Remons themselves were bolts of pure energy. Father Rock explained that this energy was much darker and denser than dark matter of the visible universe. This form of discordant frequency vibrations and energies caused cancer and harmful viruses in humankind and animals.

This same energy was the force of deterioration to the all. Remon matter was not detectable or visible at the earth realm by humans at this time. Father Rock was the only entity that could see this energy with his naked eye. Father Rock had given the secrets of the universe to Dr. C in the form of the magic dimensional language to be converted to a math form to benefit humankind and to save earth from self-destruction. This could be done by educating humankind to stand in the light of knowledge of the secrets from the beginning to the all of infinity. Knowledge of Remon energy was included in the information. The black energy changed the molecular structure of any entity and compromised the stabilization energy of the entity to create discordant frequencies and vibration. Once this discordant frequency and vibration were inconstant, the energy absorbed the outer discordant vibrations and frequencies slowly creating a cosmic vacuum, eventually and unequally absorbing and converting all entities it touched into its own vibrational frequency and form of energy. Like ripples on a pond, the discordance could spread throughout the universe if left unchecked by cosmic harmony.

Father Rock looked at Zoron and stopped talking. Zoron said, "Father Rock, what a great gift this is to all that is and shall ever be. I am honored to work with you." Zoron worried that this mission would require a lot of luck and that the odds were against him. Tink would accompany him to Remon in a similar state of suspended animation. If the computer failed, they would not be returning. "Ready?" asked Zoron. Tink said, "Yip, let's go for it." They would lift off in 24 hours. They spent the evening and night in relaxation, enjoying every quiet moment of what might be their final day with family and friends.

Father Rock waited until the last moment to do what must be done. Everyone gathered silently as Zoron and Tink were strapped into the suspended animation pods. Tears slid down Aura's cheeks, but she did not flinch. One hand rested on Toron's shoulder, the other caressed Zoron's face. "It will be fine", she said, barely above a whisper, "You'll be back in no time." She leaned in and kissed him on the lips as Father Rock made the final calculations that slowed and then stopped his heart. Her tears splashed his face as she felt his lips grow cold. She closed her eyes and rested her forehead against his chest for a moment, unwilling to raise her head and see his glazed eyes. Toron pulled her hand. He was the man of the house while dad was gone, that's what his dad had said last night. He had to take care of his mom. He had to be strong. "Mom, don't cry. It's going to be all right. Father Rock said so, and he's never wrong. Please come away so they can lift off. The sooner they go, the sooner they'll come back, right?" Aura straightened and hugged her young son. Mercifully, Zoron's eyes were closed and he looked as if he were sleeping. "You're so right darling. Daddy will be back in no time at all." Hand in hand, they exited the StarFlyer. Aura walked proudly, with her back was straight and her head was high. Only her eyes showed her terror.

The journey was flawless. The computer did exactly as programmed and lifted the suspended animation on time and then administered the medications and shocks that would restart the hearts of the two adventurers.

Zoron awoke first, then Tink. "How are you doing, little buddy?," asked Zoron. Tink adjusted his sunglasses. "Raring to go, Let's get the Claybous."

StarFlyer's computer would land the ship. When they touched down, Zoron handed Tink an equipment bag. "Suit up, lets get to work. The quicker the better, in and out." StarFlyer's door opened. The terrain was very rough, with colorful rocks or crystals all over. It was beautiful but dangerous. Dotting the landscape were pools of acid from the rains that billowed toxic smoke. The plant life was weird-looking, like long red snakes. Other plants had spade shaped leaves in clusters like large peony plants but in the middle of the plant was a clump of needle-like crystals in place of flowers. They were bright yellow in color with tiny drops of black liquid on them. Tink took his probe rod and touched the flower. It shot a crystal straight through Tink's metal rod.

"Keep that rod to yourself! Hurry," Zoron pointed to the horizon,

"See the mountain range? That's where the Claybous crystals are supposed to be located." Zoron looked back and saw a red snake plant wrapping itself around Tink.

Tink started screaming, "Get this thing off me. Yo! Yeek! It's gross." Zoron took his star gun and shot a stream of blue energy that melted the snake into quivering jelly stuff. In an instant, the mutated form of the creature had formed back into a living creature and multiplied; now there were three of them. Zoron said, "Move fast." A large acid puddle blocked their path, but it was shallow and had large flat stones sticking up. They started across, tapping each stone before stepping. About half way across, one popped open and an orange gas came out of it. He tossed a small piece of equipment into the gas and it melted. Zoron said wryly, "Great. Acid gas. Nice place."

Tink asked playfully, "Are we having fun yet?" "You're really funny," answered Zoron. "You weren't so funny when the snake plant had you." Tink was suddenly serious "Ya, that's true. Thanks for saving me, Zoron. Let's go, I don't like this place."

Distances were deceptive. They were already at the foot of the mountain. They heard a whooshing sound and a flying creature with probably a 100-foot wingspan dove at Zoron and Tink. It had large red eyes with scaly skin. The skin was bright red. Its teeth were long fangs like a snake's and the claws on its feet were at least 10 feet long and came to sharp points.

They ran past two large rocks, then saw an opening. Zoron said, "Look Tink, a cave. Let's hide in here. We need to rest." Although they had spacesuits on they were hot; hot and tired. As they rested, they looked at the walls of the cave. Tink said, "Look at these white crystals. Let's test them." He ran his tester over them and shrugged, "They're just diamonds. What a waste. They aren't good for anything." Zoron said, "I'll take a couple back for Aura. They are pretty." Tink smacked his lips. "Love love, kissie kissie." Zoron tossed a food packet at Tink's head. "Shut up, you idiot, you're like a little kid."

FATHER ROCK

Tink stuck out his tongue. "See? We *are* having fun now."

Zoron said, "Riiiight. How about we get some sleep. Maybe that thing will get bored and go away."

The flying creature was sitting outside the cave, too big to get through the small entry. It was just sitting there staring at the cave. The explorers were burnt out from the stress of the journey and the hike. They both went to sleep. As the daylight came Zoron awoke and peered outside. Tink said, "How about the creature?" Zoron said, "It's gone. Maybe it's nocturnal. Let's hit it." They started up the mountain. About halfway up they saw a flash of blinding color. There it was, a beautiful Claybous crystal. "All right," Zoron said, as he picked up the crystal, "let's go." He slipped on a rock and as he fell backward the crystal flew out of his hand and rolled down into a small crevasse in the mountain. Zoron said, "Oh no, now what?"

Tink looked over the edge. "It's ok. I can get it. I'm just the right size for this job."

Zoron cautioned him. "Its deep, be careful down there."

Tink lowered himself into the narrow crevasse. "I can shoot the crystal up to you with my slingshot." The sling was Tink's favorite toy, and he practiced every day. Snap, a perfect shot right into Zoron's hand. He tucked it into a pouch on his suit and turned to find Tink straining to get out of the crevasse. The slick sides presented a problem. Tink could not get positioned to pull himself out, and wriggling had made him slide further into the narrowing gap. He was stuck fast. "Leave me and take the crystal to Father Rock."

Zoron said, "No way, we came together and we are going to leave together. This is not time to get stupidly brave." Zoron took a can of foam out of his equipment pack and sprayed the foam around Tink's waist. He said, "Ok, now try." Tink did. "It's no good, try to wiggle." Tink tried again. Zoron said, "Grab this pack strap." As Tink took the strap, Zoron braced his feet against a big rock. One more big wiggle and a strong tug from Zoron, and Tink was free!

"Good, now back to the StarFlyer before something else happens. We are going home." As they started back a big Remon energy animal appeared. Zoron held his hand over Tink's mouth. The energy animal jumped right at them and went over Tink and Zoron's head and absorbed a flying creature that was in a large cave sleeping behind them. "Move fast," Zoron said. They got back to the StarFlyer and took off. "Man, that was a close one," Tink said. Zoron said, "You are right about that. Good job, little buddy. Good job."

"Thanks," Tink said. "Next stop, home."

A small black and red spider had slipped into an equipment bag. The spider crawled up on Tink's arm and bit him. Tink yelled, "Zawee!"

"What's wrong?" Zoron saw the spider. *Slam,* he killed it. Tink started to shake and passed out. *Oh no, what now*, Zoron thought. I don't know if this will work. He took his medical bag out. In the bag was a small blue crystal. Zoron placed it under Tink's tongue and headed at full speed for home. In about three hours Tink made a sound. "Oh, oh, I feel sick," Tink said. Zoron took another blue crystal, his last one, and put it under Tink's tongue. He was thinking to himself, *that had better work*. In about six hours Tink awoke again and said, "I feel better. I am hungry." Zoron knew his little buddy was ok, now he was ready to eat, that was a good sign.

Twenty-Nine

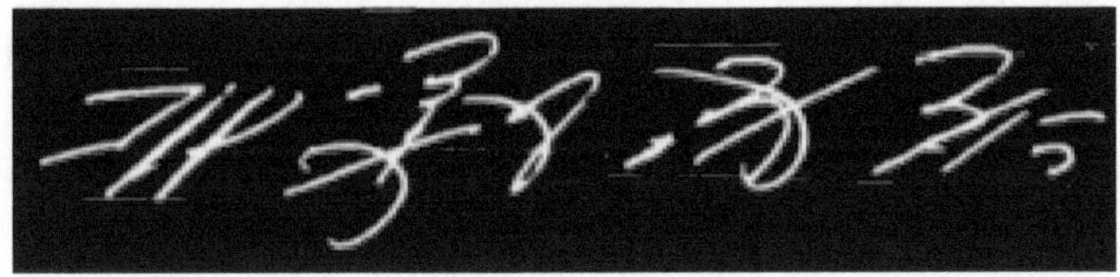

The StarFlyer landed on Galtor. Father Rock, Aura, Dr. C, Spark, Electro, Zap, Zon, were all excited to see Zoron and Tink. The Muzoids started their victory dance by buzzing all over the place, jumping and yelling. Aura grabbed Zoron and gave him a big kiss. Tink waited with his lips puckered up with his face blushing red. Aura saw him and she gave him a kiss on the cheek and said, "You're my little hero." The Muzoids whistled and said, "kissie kissie, hee, hee."

Dr. C, "Good show, bravo, pip pip cheerio." Everyone was happy. Father Rock beamed, "I am glad you're safe" and gave the guys a big hug and a pat on the back. Father Rock said, "Everyone come here." Everyone gathered around him. I have created a ring, the Unicrystal ring. It is the same design as the Unicrystal necklaces. There shall be very few of these rings presented. All of you shall receive one. This ring of honor is given because of your bravery in the wars with the evil Demos and his demons."

Everyone was overjoyed with this unicrystal ring of honor. “Good job everyone.”

Zoron said, “Look at this blue, green, yellow, purple and red Claybous crystal, it’s perfect. And it’s large enough to make four crystals for your guitar.” “Yes,” Father Rock said, “they are beautiful and of the tenth-power, fantastic work. Now let us eat and be merry. This calls for a big celebration.” The Muzoids cooked a big meal for the party. Dr. C said to Father Rock in a low voice, “Zoron said it was bad. They almost did not make it back. I’ll tell you more later. I don’t want to upset Aura.” Father Rock held up his glass and said, “WE ARE AS ONE FREQUENCY UNITED AS ONE FROM THE BEGINNING OF LIGHT TO INFINITY. WE HAVE TRANSCENDED TIME AND SPACE AS A UNIFIED FORCE FIELD. WE ARE THE ALL. AND THE ALL IS OF THE LIGHT.” Dr. C said, “Here here.”

Demos watched in his dimensional viewer. “I will show you, Father Rock. Celebrate all you want before I kill all of you. Maybe I can torment you for awhile before the kill. Oh yes, precious Aura. That’s the way to hurt you, Zoron. I almost forgot your precious Aura. I will think of something real good this time. My new demons will have fun with her. Oh, by the way, I have created some new demons from my black blood. My thick, beautiful blood. They are very mean.” Demos laughs in his deep, gravelly voice, “Ha Ha, I am coming soon.”

“Ok, everyone,” Father Rock said, “we have had a great meal thanks to the Muzoids. Let’s rest tonight and will get to work tomorrow.”

Demos says, “Hmm, what does Father Rock mean?”

The next day, Zoron said, "Father Rock, we need to prepare the Claybous crystal to fit your guitar.” Father Rock turned to Dr. C. “I need a formula to absorb light into a solid form. Here is the dimensional magic language that contains the information you need. You must translate or transpose the magic language to quantum math to allow the construction of a device to be contained in a weapon for the StarFlyer.”

Dr. C said, “Hmm very interesting theory.” Doc C said, “Light in a solid form, compressed light. Ya Ya, compressed light or condensed light." His mind raced, "Let me see." He mumbled as he walked to his lab. Tink said, "Look at the Doc, he is on cloud nine. He's got one of Father Rock's dimensional language problems." You can hear the Doc all over the place. "Ya, no, I think, no, that's not it, hmm." Spark said, "Ya, he's on cloud nine for sure."

Father Rock continued, "Muzoids, I need the greatest battleship ever built. We shall call it StarFlyer 2. This ship must be your best, fastest, strongest, with the biggest weapon capacity possible. We must be able to chase Demos down if he tries to transfer his evil black energy from Zander's body to a new human capsule." The Muzoids started to work. Zap said, "Boys, we got to get to work fast." Zon started to draw up some new designs for S.F. 2.

"Aura," Father Rock said, "contact all the TUW. We need their assistance again. TUW has over one billion members now. Aura, get the best in each field. We need some space engineers, ship builders to help the Muzoids. Just select the members now don't alert them about Demos. We don't want Demos getting word we know he is alive." Aura said, "ok," and gave Father Rock a hug. Father Rock picked up his guitar and started creating some new runs.

In the cave, the cult chanted "Demos, Demos." Demos and the cult were dressed in black robes with hoods pulled over their heads. Demos took out a whip and started whipping the demons. He was screaming, "Make me a new death ray and keyboard or I will feed you to my 12-headed pet dragon." He laughed in his deep, evil roar. "I want subsonic and ultrahigh frequencies. Make this one twice as powerful as the last." He whipped another demon urging, "Hurry you fools, hurry."

Toron was playing in the small pyramid in the backyard when the demon arrived to kidnap Aura. The demon could not get to Aura inside the sanctuary, but he could get to Toron. Toron was waving at his mother when a black energy engulfed him. Aura yelled, "Run Toron." It was too late. The demon lifted him in the air and they disappeared. Aura screamed out, “Zoron, Demos took Toron.”

Everyone ran outside. A voice filled the air, “Father Rock! Yes, it’s me, your old buddy Demos. Ha Ha. I have Toron and I am going to kill him, maybe today or in a week, it depends on my mood. I am in charge now, am I not?” His laugh faded into the sunshine, leaving the team stunned and silent.

"Toron", Demos said, “you little brat, are you afraid of me?” “No and you’re a jerk. When my grandfather gets a hold of you, he will make toast out of you.” “Hmm, feisty little brat. He’s no fun.” Demos went back to work with his cult. Toron yelled at his retreating back, “You are still a jerk!” Demos answered, “I have some surprises for Father Rock, you shall see.”

Zoron entered Toron’s energy code in his Digimoid computer and hit Search. The back azimuth read NASA. “Toron could be in the Code Room. It‘s a secure facility and Zander can get access.” Dr. C said. “You’re probably right, Doc,” said Zoron. “We must go to NASA.” Quickly, they made preparations. It was decided that a small team was necessary to slip in and out quietly. The logical choices were Zoron and Dr. C, since they had many connections with NASA scientists and their presence would not be remarkable. They transported to a quiet storage area. “Now to the Code Room. Lots of guards but I have a Sleeptor.” The Doc took out a small device and shot the guards. A red and green light spread vibratory frequencies of peace and put all the guards to sleep in seconds. Dr. C nodded. “They will be out for a while. We have about one hour. “

Zoron said, “That should give us enough time to break the code. This *must* work.” He took out his decoder and worked furiously. “Now I think I have it. Yes! That’s got it, we are in.” As Zoron opened the door, he ducked a flying stapler, which was followed by a hurtling boy wielding a clipboard in a furious attack. "Wait! He yelled, fending off the blows

"Toron, it's me, it's Dad, stop hitting me!" Toron opened his tightly clenched eyes and dropped the fearsome weapon to hug his rescuer. Zoron chuckled "That's my boy. How brave you are to attack Demos with office supplies! Thank God, you're ok."

Toron jumped up and down. "Oh boy, I knew you would come. Are we going to battle Demos now?"

Zoron ruffled his son's hair. "Soon, sport. First, we will put everything back so Demos will think you are still a prisoner. The guards will wake in a few minutes. They won't remember any of this. Let's get out of here. I can't wait to see Aura's face when she sees you. Zander can't go in the Code Room too often himself without raising suspicion, so he will not know you have been rescued. We have the edge on Demos now."

They transported back to Galtor. Aura saw Toron and ran to him and said, "My baby is home. Oh thank God, he is home." Father Rock gave Toron a big hug. The Muzoids did their victory dance. Father Rock said, "Time is running out. I'd love to celebrate the rescue, but we must get back to work." The Team Leaders dispersed to their various tasks. A couple of hours later, Zoron came in with the Claybous crystal cut to fit Father Rock's guitar. Zoron said, "Fire up your guitar, Father Rock." Father Rock put the crystal in the guitar and said, "Ok, I am ready." He stood on the stage and played a run. "It's powerful…real powerful." Lasers shot all over the place in mixed colors. "Wow! Look at that," said Dr. C. "It's awesome. Claybous has got the stuff and Father Rock is the greatest guitarist there is or ever has been or will ever be."

Thirty

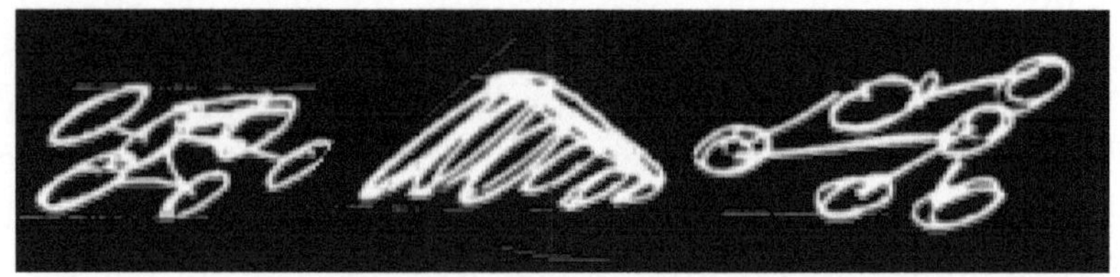

"I am ready for you, Demos. Now I shall destroy you," Father Rock yelled as he blasted wild runs on his guitar. "I have transcended time and space to the now of your existence Demos, and I shall kill you." The Muzoids were working on StarFlyer 2. It was almost completed and it looked like a winner, a super powerful ship with laser weapons and dimensional transcender capabilities. "We will zap them dead, ha ha." Spark said, "We'll make toast out of them."

Father Rock gathered them all into his cosmic energy room to pull maximum dimensional energy. The room was full of colored pyramid crystals. A recording of Father Rock's music played, celestial, peaceful music. In another room a solid crystal guitar was on display, shimmering with ethereal beauty. It was cosmic blue and diamond white. Father Rock played this guitar with his mind energies, projecting frequencies to the instrument. Its sound included the subsonic and ultrasonic frequencies that align all existing things from earth to infinity. This music balanced the one-cycle energy pulse of all living organisms. The guitar that Father Rock had played to fight Demos dealt with only earth realms: mind, body and soul. Father Rock closed his eyes and the room filled with light. And the all was love, love and light. Everyone was unified as one energy. Father Rock said, “I shall recite a poem I wrote.

Ever-Changing Life

To transform into what is
Unknown
To be part of the magic of
Life
Sometimes I wonder and
Remember you
In a different form
And you say to me
And I say to you
But we don’t hear
It doesn’t matter
Because we have traveled
In the same light beam
Before we came here
This feeling is genetic
From the center of the
Universe to infinity
Before time was time
Before this planet was here
We are all what is called
Energy
An ever-changing
Mass of life.”

The Team Leaders were moved very deeply by the poem. Father Rock said, “All the universal frequencies are as one. I am ready to face Demos.”

Thirty-One

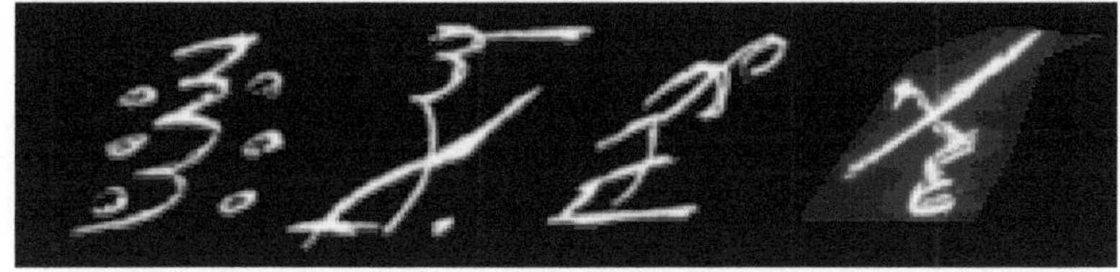

It was time to finalize strategies for battle. Everyone was ready. They all stood on the time transporter and, *bam*, the travelers were on earth. The team looked at the site. It was much different than the last one, higher mountains, very large rocks. A large lake rippled in the deep valley region. A river led to the lake area, and tall trees and thick brush grew in the other parts of the range. There were several caves and small springs. Father Rock said, “Hide the StarFlyer in the large cave. Put bombs in the trees and mines in the river at points A B C, also place C4 compound under the bridges. Dr. C, how about the light condenser?”

Dr. C said, “Close but not quite ready, sir.”

“I will need the condensed light added to the nano tubes to bust Demos’ death ray.” Everyone wore their unicrystal necklaces. “We have the good power of the light force to destroy all evil. You are the cosmic soldiers of the universes and all dimensions, the time travelers carrying the power of the light force to the all. We must destroy Demos.“ Everyone clapped and cheered. “We are the freedom fighters.” “Ya ya, the freedom fighters.” Aura had called Frankie to prepare the battlefield. As soon as he arrived, he started to organize things. He quickly made a list of the personnel he would need from the TUW for the big battle.

Demos viewed them. “Hmm, Frankie is in this again, you brought him in. Well I must kill him first. Then the team will fall apart and fold without his expert direction.”

Dr. C announced, “I have condensed light; here it is, Father Rock.” Dr. C held a nano tube in the air. The tube had a black cover on it. It was so powerful that it would blind someone in one-tenth of a second. Father Rock said, “I shall call it the cosmic light. Yes, that is it, the cosmic light.” Dr. C beamed with pride. “Ha ha, hee hee, that’s me, Dr. C.”

Zoron pulled his secret equipment pack out and opened it. Zoron saw the note from Baxter, “Remember the olives. HAHA.” “Hey, Nerdboy super glued my equipment together. I will get even with him after this mess is over.” Zoron shook his head and laughed saying, “Baxter. Olives, oh boy.”

Spark informed Father Rock that the StarFlyer 2 work was done. Father Rock said, “Let’s give the ship a test flight.” Spark said, “I will be the pilot.” Father Rock said, “No, you won’t, I shall pilot, you are too crazy. You can be my co-pilot.” Spark said, “Ok you’re the boss.” Toron looked up from his computer game. “Grandpa, can I come on the test flight?” “Absolutely,” Father Rock answered. “Let’s go!” *Zoom*, the ship took off.

The StarFlyer 2 was a round, disc-shaped ship. It became invisible upon command. It was the fastest ship ever built. Also it changed color to match its surroundings. Father Rock said, “Now I will try the laser weapons.” *Blast!* It was awesome. Then he hit the red button on the control panel. That was the energy sponge that Dr. C designed to absorb the evil black energy. This way if Demos discharges his black energy out of Zander’s body, we will get him and destroy him. He will pay dearly for taking Dr. C's grandson."

Toron asked, "Grandpa, what was that mass of blue and black energy we passed?" "It is called Perseus A." "What kind of sound would it make if we could hear it?" "Well, you cannot hear its sound yet. Later, you will receive the power to do so, but for now, you cannot. Perseus A makes sounds waves. It is a guttural melody in B-Flat, fifty-seven octaves below middle-C and a million billion times deeper than the limits of human hearing." "Wow, that's wild! Do you play that sound on your guitar?" "Yes, when I play universal music. The parts you hear are but a small part of my cosmic musical scale. I play all that is, the all of everything that exists. I set the frequencies that balance all existing things." "Wow", Toron said, his blue eyes sparkling, "That's why Demos wants to kill you, so he can break the balance?" "Yes, he would disrupt the universal harmonies, sending discordant waves throughout the all, throwing everything into a chaos he would rule." Toron nodded slowly. "We can't let him do that."

"Grandpa, is it true that a planet called Neptune has diamonds on it?" "Yes, Toron, beneath the 1,200 MPH winds that move the clouds on Neptune, there is a hard rain of diamonds created from the compressed boiling ocean of methane when the diamonds fall towards the planet's core. Friction is created and makes the power of the storm. This explains why Neptune generates 2.6 times more energy than it receives from the sun." "Could we go get some Neptune diamonds someday?" "Sure, but right now I should get back to work, ok? We'll be flying pretty fast and there won't be much to see, so why don't you sign on to that Kerb game you like. I know you enjoy that." "Great idea, Grandpa, I love PR. My friends on the forum are from all over the world. I can't wait to tell them about diamonds from Neptune." Father Rock waved his hand distractedly, "Have fun Toron. When I have time I will tell you all about the invisible universe and dark matter."

Demos growled, “Hurry up with my battleship.” The cult chanted “Demos Demos.” Demos summoned his favorite demon. Dreg appeared, 10 feet tall, 500 pounds of muscles. His skin was a bright, slimy, ugly-looking yellow-mustard color and he had powerful wings with which to fly. He had gills in his neck to stay under water for long periods of time. Dreg had long fingernails and fang-like teeth. The fangs had poison in them that absorbed energy. Dreg’s fire-red eyes hypnotized anyone that he looked at. Dreg could run faster than any animal and jump tremendous distances. He was the demon of all demons. Demos knew that Dreg was hard to deal with and that he must watch him. Dreg was out for himself. Demos said, “Father Rock is my target.” Dreg said, “What is in it for me?” Demos said, “I shall give you all the power of the darkness; of course not as much as I have, but much more than you possess now.” Dreg said, “I want one other thing, Aura. She has delicious energy.” Demos said, “No, she is mine.” Dreg said, “Fine, I am leaving.” He turned to leave. Demos said, “Ok, you have a deal but only after we have killed all of them. Then you can have Aura.” The Vibor demons were unhappy that Dreg would be in charge. They did not trust or like Dreg; as a matter of fact, they hated him.

Demos and Dreg headed for the mountaintop. Dreg dove in the river and said, “They put mines in the river. Well, I have a few tricks of my own, like my proton slicer that will melt them all with one blast. I will place this in the river. That will fix them.” Dreg screamed as the Vibor demons got ready for battle, “If you make any mistakes I will kill you myself.”

Aura said, “I don’t want grandfather to fight again.” Zoron said, “Don’t worry about him. He is strong and he will win the battle.” Zoron left for the lab. Toron said to Aura, “I want to help.” Aura said, “You can take this disc to your father, he forgot it.”

“Dad, here is the disc. I want to help you fight Demos. How can I help?” “Just sit here and watch the screen. Let me know if any of these red blips move past the line right here, that‘s extremely important. That will tell us if any demons are sneaking up."

Demos' voice said to Father Rock, "Do you miss your little angel, Toron, your great-grandchild that I own?"

Father Rock smiled, but did not answer the taunt. "*Good, he hasn't been back to the Code Room, so he thinks he still has Toron prisoner", he* thought.

Demos said, "Oh by the way, I am going to kill Toron before your eyes, Father Rock."

Father Rock took out the small box that Bill and he found when he was a young boy. It was time to use the power of the blue energy in the box again. Father Rock lay back and placed his hand on the box. Blue energy shot up the length of Father Rock's arm. He started to glow as the blue energy traveled up the veins in his body. He glowed white-blue energy with a purple afterglow. His body levitated about one foot over the bed. His body changed colors as it absorbed different energy frequencies. After five hours, his body slowly descended to the bed and Father Rock was fully energized. He awoke and felt rested. As he started to get up out of bed he could feel the heat energy in his hands. He put his hands about one foot apart and a blue energy orb formed. The orb floated in the air then another orb appeared; it was purple. He lifted his hands and it also floated in the air. "*They are so beautiful,*" Father Rock thought, "*it's like a dream state.*" After a few minutes the air was full of different colored energy orbs. The room glowed soft colors and sparks of energy floated among the orbs. As Father Rock moved, all the energy in the room slowly moved around him. He projected his mind energy to the solid crystal and the guitar began to play a cosmic music. It was peaceful, spiritual music and Father Rock danced. As he danced he slowly changed colors and levitated off the floor. He was in a deep trance. Father Rock became the energy and the energy became Father Rock. Aura opened the door and she was breathless at this beautiful sight. Aura did not want to disturb Father Rock, so she just watched for a long while and then quietly closed the door.

Thirty-Two

Demos' battleship was complete. It was called the Scorpion. Demos bragged that the Scorpion could take the StarFlyer any day. "I have the death ray installed and the best pilot in the universe, me, and Dreg is my co-pilot." The Scorpion had a tail that curled up over its back. When deployed, it would swing out and shoot the death ray. Demos' ship also had negative energy bombs containing Remon energy animals that would latch onto their target and melt or dissolve it instantly.

The TUW has been notified: divers, engineers, tech people, computer experts, skateboarders, bike riders, the whole TUW team had been called in. Most of the team were involved the last battle, so they were combat vets ready to go. Jibe walked up to Frankie and said "All the TUW team arrived during the middle of the night. In twenty-four hours, we will have the battlefield ready." Very quickly large speakers were set up to blast Father Rock's guitar at Demos. Frankie set large crystals up on both sides of the stage and hid some remote crystals and speakers throughout the battlefield.

Dreg too, was almost set up. He put poison snakes in pits so the team members would fall and get bitten by the snakes. Dreg put a camouflage canvas over the battleship Scorpion.

The Muzoids were busy calling the dimensional transcenders and setting booby traps. The dive team was camped by the river, in hiding, waiting for the battle to start. The climbers would come over the back side of Demos' mountain and try to hit Demos with a sneak attack.

Dreg had placed water serpents in the river and the lake. He put the Vibor demons underground. Their job would be to shoot up out of the ground and attack the Muzoids.

All was ready at dusk. Soon after the sun went down over the mountain the battle would begin. However something weird was going on; neither Father Rock nor Demos had ordered their troops to engage. Tink said, "What is up?" Zoron said, "I don't know, Tink. Father Rock and Demos are just staring at one another across the mountain range." Their eyes were locked. Father Rock's white-hot eyes shot a focused beam at Demos. Demos stared back at Father Rock with his evil eyes shooting a red energy beam back at Father Rock. The white energy and red energy collided in the middle of the battlefield, exploding in slow motion, throwing off waves of energies and vibrations and colors in a spectacular display of power. These masters of good and evil would fight for all of the universes and dimensions to infinity. Yet the night passed and Father Rock and Demos had not moved. The sun started to rise and still they glared in a trance at one another. "This waiting is killing me," Zoron said.

"Just wait for Father Rock to signal us." Dr. C was restless as well, but he knew the timing had to be just right. Father Rock stood with his guitar in a playing position. Demos stood with his hand on the keyboard of his instrument.

The mountain team had used the time to go over the mountain and come up behind Demos. They appeared behind Demos' stage and flashed a crystal to signal Father Rock that they were in position. Dreg ran on stage to warn Demos. *Wham!* Father Rock fired a blast at Demos. At last, the battle was on! Demos fought back with his death ray. Spark called on the D.T.s, “Shoot a ball of fire at Demos.” It missed and fried one of Demos’ speakers to a crisp. Zon spread nano chips on the rocks next to Demos’ stage. The nano D.T.s melted the rocks and the rocks crushed the stage. “Take that,” said Zon. *Wap*, there went the stage. About one-fifth of the stage was gone.

Demos was furious. “Zon, take this.” *Wam*! Demos shot a death ray at Zon and hit the rock he was standing on. Just before the rock crumbled Zon jumped into the air and rolled down the side of the mountain. Zon said, “You missed me.” Demos went crazy and blasted the death ray all over the mountain range in a fit of anger. Zon did a little Muzoid victory dance. That made Demos even more furious, if that were possible. A Vibor popped up out of the ground, hitting Zon on the head with a weapon of some kind. It knocked Zon down. Electro said, “I don’t think so,” hitting the Vibor with one of his power shocks, killing it instantly.

Electro grabbed Zon and carried him down the side of a small hill saying, “Let’s go, little buddy.” His little legs were going fast as they could. All kinds of lasers exploded around them. Father Rock witnessed the action and said, “Those Muzoids are hot stuff, real fighters.” Zon’s eyes were open and his head bounced up and down as Electro ran, carrying him over his shoulder.

Father Rock fired a big blast of red energy and guitars runs of screaming sound at Demos. Father Rock spun around in a circle, white hair flying in the air like wild bolts of electricity changing colors, screaming, “Demos, I shall kill you.” The blue, red, white, purple laser energy was hitting everything. Trees and rocks were cut in half as Father Rock glowed with white-hot energy. Colors of red, green, purple streamed up and down his body. Father Rock shot a beam of light. It streaked ahead and hit very close to Demos. Demos fired back.

Father Rock shot fire from his eyes and mouth and threw balls of light orbs at Demos. Demos put up a shield to block the orbs, but two of them got to Demos. He jumped into a safety pit at the front of the stage, but the orbs were so strong that when they exploded they knocked Demos out. About ten minutes passed. Demos slowly awakened. He pulled himself back to the keyboard and played a monster chord, a deep, roaring sound. He laughed and said, "Take that, Father Rock." A flying demon swooped down at Father Rock. Father Rock spun around and blasted the demon from the sky. *Zing*, it was blown to pieces.

Demos roared in frustration. The time had come to show just how cruel he could be. At his command, the demons pulled the covering from a huge viewing screen. "Watch this, Father Rock. Watch your precious Toron die before your eyes. I'll kill him slowly and enjoy his screams." The scene on the viewer faded to an outside view of the code room at NASA. Tiny snake demons slithered all over the ground. As the Team Leaders stood mesmerized, the door was opened by a guard whose wooden movements indicated a deep trance. They snakes breached the threshold slithering over each other in their haste to get to their victim. "I picked the smallest ones just for you, Father Rock. They will bite Toron in a thousand places, each delivering a tiny amount of poison. He will die in horrible, screaming agony. Unless, of course, you'd like to die in his place and end this now. It's not too late. Just say it. I give up, Demos. You are the Master of the All."

Father Rock grinned. "I don't think so Demos." He winked at Toron, who was watching the screen with big round eyes.

The view screen switched to an inside shot of the empty Code Room. Demos smiled evilly. "Toron cannot hide from my demons. They can sense him. In a moment, they will find him and....NOOOOOOOOOOOO….." The screen went black and TUW watched Demos cavort in impotent rage on his stage.

Toron laughed happily. "Guess we showed him, didn't we Grandpa?" Father Rock ruffled his hair. "We did indeed, my boy, we did indeed."

Furiously, Demos shot a blast of black energy at Frankie in the Command Center. Aura was there with Dr. C. Frankie was hurt and fell to the floor. Aura ran to Frankie and said, "Dr. C, can you run the fire direction center guidance system?"

"Oh, well, sure I can." Aura said, "do it. I'll give Frankie first aid." His leg was bleeding and his hand and head were cut. Dr. C yelled, "Got ya." *Bang!* "Got another one of the nasty demons." Aura tried to stop Frankie's bleeding and bring him back to consciousness.

Dr. C was really pounding the demons as he turned his Irish beret backward on his head. "I say, come and get it, you black-hearted fools." A flying demon hit the window of the control center and shattered it, sending glass all over the team members inside. A sliver caught Dr. C in the face, cutting a jagged path across his forehead and down the side, narrowly missing his left eye. Blood poured down his face, but Dr. C kept firing his Jirow weapon, blasting into the demon's chest plate. The demon, with half its body still hanging out of the window, made a high, screeching sound and whipped his head back and forth, trying to wriggle farther in to the room. Dr. C saw his chance when the demon's head lifted and shot up into its exposed throat. *Bam! Bam! Bam!* "Righto, ha ha, hee hee, it's me, Dr. C." Dr. C shoved the dying demon backwards and heard it thump on the dirt outside. "I say," Dr. C yelled cheerfully, wiping the slime from his hands, "Pleasure doing business with you, old boy." He washed the blood from his face and took the pipe from his pocket. "I could certainly do with a cup of tea," he remarked to an astonished Aura.

Electro had Zon back on his feet. Can't keep a good trooper down, especially a freedom fighter. "TUW all the way," Zon shouted defiantly. Zon, Electro, Zap, Tink, Spark tapped away on their Digimoids computers, calling all kinds of dimensional transcenders. The battle raged on. Zap ordered Freezon to freeze the Vibors. He called his D.T. sound blast, a searing sound. The Vibors started to shake and make a gurgling sound and then exploded into a thousand pieces. "You're toast," he said, "Tee Hee Hee."

FATHER ROCK

Frankie came around and said, "Doc C, looks like you're having the time of your life." Dr. C said, "Righto, the old war, you know. Yip, he almost got me." Dr. C gave Frankie a sharp salute. Frankie said, "Good job, Doc. I will take over now." "Yes, thank you, sir." Tink ran in the door. "Father Rock is hit and Demos is hit; they fired and hit each other. They are both down." Tink waved his arms in the air and jumped up and down.

Zoron said, "Tink, are they dead?" "No, no, ah, both of them are just wounded and unconscious. The fighting was fierce and it just stopped on both sides. No one knows what to do."

Father Rock was taken to the cave and Demos was taken to the Scorpion. Zoron said, "In four hours it will be daylight. Right now our top priority is Father Rock." Zoron, Aura and Dr. C went into the cave. Everyone else stayed on watch. The cult surrounded Demos, chanting, "Demos, Demos our master."

Zoron said, "Get Zap to get me a full battle report." About ten minutes later Zap came in with the report. "We have killed 16,742 Vibor demons."

"How about Dreg?" "No, Dreg is still alive and with Demos. We lost 10,521 and 8,221 TUW's are wounded and we lost 12 D.T.s. Two Muzoids were wounded but are able to fight." Zoron said, "This has been much more difficult than the last battle." A Vibor demon suddenly shot up through the floor. Aura turned around with a pistol she had grabbed off the table and fired; *bang, bang, bang,* three shots in the Vibor. Another popped up behind her and she spun around. One shot, *bang*, straight in the head. Both demons slumped to the floor, dead. Dr. C said, "Good show, Aura."

Thirty-Three

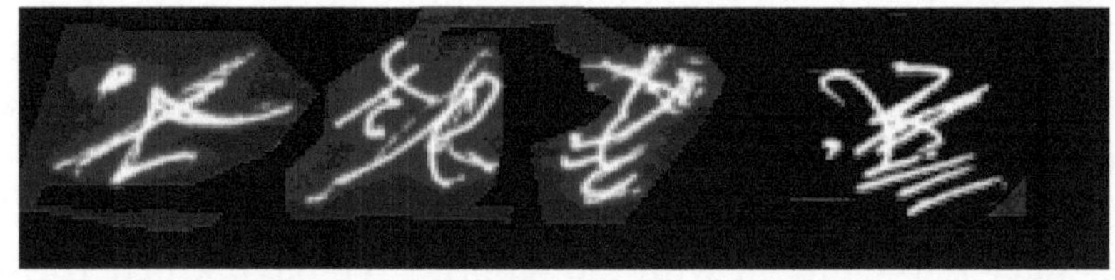

Zoron said, “Dr. C, I don’t know how much more the Muzoids can take. They are outnumbered a thousand to one.” Dr. C said, “I know. We might have to use the cosmic light. Something’s got to give and soon.” Father Rock opened his eyes and said, “Demos, is he dead?”

“He’s wounded. Dreg has taken him into the Scorpion.”

Father Rock‘s shoulders slumped, “Oh no.”

Dr. C said, “Zoron, I need to examine him.“ Zoron nodded and shooed everyone else outside. Dr. C looked Father Rock over and said, “The low frequency shot from Demos hit him and broke a couple of ribs. He is in lots of pain, but main thing is that his hands are not hurt, he can still play his guitar. Bring his guitar by his bed, please. This way he will feel comfortable.” Father Rock put his hand on the guitar and fell asleep.

Zoron said, “He just needs rest.” They took turns watching over him as he slumbered.

FATHER ROCK

Demos awoke in the Scorpion and growled, "Did I kill him, Dreg?" "No, he is still alive." His red eyes glowed with anger and slowly closed as he mumbled I will kill him, I will." Demos fell into a deep sleep. The cult chanted, "Demos, Demos."

Dr. C took Toron so Aura and Zoron could be alone for a while. Zoron said, "I almost forgot, I brought you something from Remon." Zoron pulled the two diamonds from his pocket. "Aren't they beautiful?" Aura said, "Yes, oh yes." "They are about thirty carats each." Zoron said, "They sparkle like your eyes." Aura smiled and said, "Zoron, you are so good to me." They were so tired they fell asleep.

Dr. C called on an old friend. John was from China. He was known as an expert in Chinese herbal medicine. Dr. C asked him to treat Father Rock. John said, "I will make a blend of my magic nectar. It will bring Father Rock's strength back fast." He opened his box of herbs and pulled out a pinch of this, a dab of that; he continued to mix about ten herbs carefully. "The Chi is perfect." He put the mixture into a small, heavy, metal black pot that had been handed down through his family for one thousand years. "The Chi of the metal has a lot to do with the healing power of the magic nectar. Give him two caps every two hours, also place this seed under his tongue each time you give him the nectar." John said, "He will be fine and much stronger than he was before." Dr. C said, "Thank you for coming." "It is my honor," John replied.

Toron said, "I was looking at the StarFlyer. There are big speakers on the front of the ship." Zoron said, "That's so Father Rock can play concerts in outer space and balance the harmonic frequencies of all existing things to create a positive force. Demos tries to disrupt Father Rock's positive music force with his vibrations of his evil music and break the universal balance."

Toron said, "I got it, he's just plain bad news. Can I see grandfather?" Zoron nodded. "He's awake, come in."

"Little one, come over here," Father Rock said. Toron said, "Gee, I though you were dead." "No, I am fine, just resting." "Dad told me how you could play that guitar and balance the universe. That's great. You got to stop that Demos."

"Soon I shall be after Demos."

Zoron motioned towards the door, "Ok, that's enough. Let him rest." "Ok, bye grandpa." Toron gave Father Rock a hug, and added, "You really are a GREAT Grandpa!", then left. Father Rock closed his eyes and went back to sleep and dreamed of energy orbs floating over a pristine lake. The orbs were a delicate pearlescent gold and seem to be lit from within. In his dream, Father rock stands on the edge of the lake with his arms held out, summoning the gold orbs. When the orbs touch him, they melt into his skin, causing his body to glow at the contact spot, until his entire body glows with a vibrant energy.

"The Vibors are moving around now," Tink said. "I will watch them close and let you know what they are up to." *Zig, bang, wap*, the Vibors were shooting at the Muzoids. The Muzoids and Frankie returned heavy fire at the Vibors. *Boom, Zow*, and big fireballs blasted at the Vibors. Spark said, "Take that, you bunch of slime." Eleven Vibors were killed and eight more wounded. "We have three wounded. They are D.T.s; they will make it ok." The battle was raging with massive fire fights, explosions, and lasers blowing debris up all over the place. The Vibors started coming out of the ground. They shot straight up in the air about ten feet and shot at the Muzoids.

A team member named Wild Bill charged into the fray, crushing one vibor after another, yelling, "I'll snap you like twigs, demons! I'll punch your eyes out and shove 'em in your mouths!" Wild Bill was a fierce warrior, 6 ft. 4 and 350 pounds of muscle, strong as a bull. *Bam!* He busted a vibor right in the head. *Splat!* "That'll teach ya!" The vibors shrank back out of his reach. "Come on, the bunch of you!" Wild Bill screamed and charged a group of fleeing demons. *Zam! Crunch! Whap!* Fearlessly, he pounded the demons. They twisted and hissed, trying to strike, but Wild Bill was too powerful. He laughed and taunted them, "You vibors fight like a bunch of sissy boys! Bring it on! Yes sir, bring it on! I'm ready to rock and roll! Is that all you got?" He grabbed the nearest demon by its tail and swung it off the side of the mountain. Wild Bill looked around. He'd cleared the area, there were no live vibors within his reach. He shot a thumbs up at the Muzoids and swooped off back down the trail in search of more demons.

A thunderous sound shook the earth and the air resounded with the roar of bombs exploding. *Bam*! A rock hit close to the cave.

The sound woke Father Rock. He asked, "Is Demos dead?" Zoron said, "No. He is in the Scorpion."

Father Rock got to his feet. "Get me in the StarFlyer. I am going after Demos. Zoron, you're my co-pilot." Spark ran into the cave yelling, "Demos just took off in the Scorpion. He's on the run. Let's get to the StarFlyer." They ran for the ship and powered it up. *Zoom*! They took off.

Father Rock said, "Zoron, have you got him on the Digi yet?" "No." "There he is, about ten grids ahead. Get a lock on him."

"I've almost got a lock. Yes. There it is. Demos is in lock. Should I fire?"

Father rocked yelled into his helmet mike. "Let him go, he is too close to earth for us to blast him now. Full speed ahead. He is going to Remon. We must stop them before he breaks the Remon barrier."

Back on Earth the battle raged on and on. The Team was powerful and proving what great warriors they really were. The Muzoids were full of energy and putting their heat on the battlefield. Zap, Spark and Electro lined up and shot blasts at the flying demons. *Wap*! *Zam*! "You got one," said Zap. "Sure did," Electro said. "Watch out behind you," yelled Spark. *Wom*! *Wom*! *Zing*! He let loose with a blast of scatter bombs. "How about that?" "You're just a show-off," Zon said, laughing. A flying serpent demon dove from the sky at Spark. Spark, Zon and Electro fired shots at the serpent demons. "You're toast," yelled Spark. The demon exploded in midair, raining funky green slime and demon chunks all over the Muzoids. "GROSS!" Spark yelled, dodging a falling eyeball. "This stuff reeks!" The

Muzoids dashed over to a team of firefighters who were busy putting out fires and said, “Hose us down boys we stink.”

The divers returned from looking for Dreg. The leader of the divers said, “We had Dreg in our sights and *bam*!, he was gone, like he disappeared.”

A Vibor demon burst into the Control Room. The demon fired a shot at Aura and Frankie. Frankie returned fire, *pow*!, right in the center of the demon’s head. “Good one,” Aura said. Another serpent demon slid into the Control Room unnoticed with all the action going on. It wrapped itself around the wires in the control panel and shorted the control board out. Weapon fire blasted all over the place. Aura said, “What’s wrong?” Frankie said, “I don’t know.” Aura lifted the panel door open and screamed, “Look, a serpent demon.” Frankie grabbed a tube of blue nano chips and threw the tube on the serpent demon. The nanos ate the serpent demon up fast. “Well, he is a dead little fried snake now, anyone for snake burgers?” Frankie laughed.

Frankie found a new panel and popped the burnt panel out. Then he popped the new one in and turned it on. He said, “We are good to go. Nice try, demon.” The battle raged on with more heavy fire coming in. The Team fought back.

Father Rock and Zoron were in hot pursuit of Demos and Dreg. Dreg pulled out a device and put it in the control panel of the Scorpion. Dreg, laughing, said, “This will fix them.” Dreg hit a button and black energy came zooming out of the Scorpion at the speed of light, right at the StarFlyer. Zoron said, “Well let’s see if Dr. C’s cosmic light works.” Father Rock hit the red button. Bingo, the black shield worked. The black energy was neutralized.

Dreg asked, “What happened? They destroyed the black energy.” Demos said, “That is impossible, nothing is more powerful than my black energy.” “They must have invented a new weapon.” “Well, try the cobon bomb.” “They are too close to us. It will kill us along with them.” “Shoot the cobon at Earth." Dreg refused flatly. "No. My Aura is there. That is the only reason I am here. Consuming her energy will make me immortal." Instead, he fired the cobon bomb into outer space. Demos was furious. He grabbed Dreg by the neck and said, "When I am done killing Father Rock, I am going after you. Just you and me, buddy." "Let go of my neck, Demos." Demos snarled, "Ok, but you're mine later." Dreg said, "We shall see who kills who." "Hit our super buster for more speed; do it now, I said," Demos screamed orders at Dreg in anger.

"Dreg said, "Your demons on Earth will soon die. We took all of their black energy source with us and the Muzoids will kill them easily." Demos said, "So what? They mean nothing to me. They are dirt under my feet. I can always make new demons from my black blood, you stupid fool." "Don't call me a stupid fool or we will forget about your precious battle and we will fight right now." Demos mumbled in a low voice, "You're a stupid fool, Dreg, and I am going to kill you slowly so you suffer." Demos said loudly, "We must get back to Remon."

Dreg said, "Demos, look, an asteroid. We could try to hide there. Shut off the power and let's hope Father Rock passes us. Let's try it." They eased the Scorpion down on the asteroid.

Zoron said, "I lost them." "Try searching for Dreg. Dreg puts out a magnetic field. He cannot control it." Father Rock said, "Search at twelve zintrons, this should locate them."

On Earth, something odd was happening. Spark said, "The Vibors are slowing down." Electro nodded. "Ya, I thought so, too, wonder what's wrong with them. They look like they are losing their energy." Zon said, "In two hours we will hit them with everything we've got."

Father Rock said, "Zoron, have you located Demos yet?" Zoron answered without taking his eyes off the screen. "No not yet." Suddenly, *Zoom*, a death ray whizzed by them. Zoron shouted, "They are behind us." Father Rock hands flew over the controls. "Hit the energy shield now."

"Got it just in time. That last shot would have finished us for sure." "I wonder how the Team is doing on Earth." Father Rock was worried for their safety. Zoron nodded. "I hope they are ok." He thought of Aura and Toron.

On Earth the time had come for the big push. "Ok, let them have everything you got." The Muzoids called all the dimensional transcenders they had. Freezon, Sleeptor, E-tor and Meltor all at once created total chaos on the battlefield. They ripped away at the Vibor demons. Demons were freezing, burning, falling asleep and being drained of energy at the same time. They fired up the big crystal. The sky lit up with explosions, lasers flashing, the night ablaze. Such a savage war this was. Green, purple, red, white-hot energy bounced all over, so overpowering. It was as if the whole earth was caught in a tornado of fire and explosions. Everything shook and rumbled from the intense bombardment in this war of good versus evil. The D.T.s were taking orders for battle from the Muzoids. They were tap, tap, tapping on their Digimoid computers, doing their Muzoid dance, jumping, laughing, and screaming all at once. "Yeah, take that!" *Zingo*! "Got ya, dirt bag." *Zow*! *Bang*! "Hee Ha Hee Hee," Dr. C chimed in as he yelled, "Right you are, take that. You black hearted demons." Doc blasted a couple more of the serpent demons. Spark set off all the bombs in the river at one time. *Boom*! Rocks started to hit the Control Room. The serpent demons hid in a small cave next to the Control Room. There were about 50 of them as they charged the Control Room. Spark said, looking from the corner of the building, "Demons at two o'clock." Dr. C, Aura, and Frankie started blasting straight-away at the serpents. One after another, the demons fell. The Muzoids joined them and opened fire on the demons; what a war machine the Team was! The smoke cleared and Demos' demons were all dead. "Yeah! Victory." The Muzoids did their famous victory dance. Dr. C did a little Irish dance step or two himself, saying, "Good show, gang, good show." He was singing "Ho Ho Hee Hee, its me, Dr. C."

FATHER ROCK

Dreg said in his gravelly, deep voice, “All the demons on earth are dead. Now it’s just the four of us left. This is the final battle that decides the Ruler Of The Universe.” Demos wanted try to hit the StarFlyer with all six of the rockets in one spot. Dreg said, “I don’t think that is a good idea.” Demos said, “We still have the death ray.” Dreg said “Fine, it’s your mistake if it doesn’t work and for now you’re the master. Set rockets 1-2-3-4-5-6,” Dreg flipped the switches on Go. “At your command.” “Fire,” Demos said. “On the way over,” Dreg answered, tracking the gauges, “impact in 4 minutes and 30 seconds.”

Zoron said, “six bogies on the way, ETA is 4 minutes, 25 seconds.” Father Rock said, “Contact Aura.” Zoron keyed his mike. “Aura, Zoron over.” “Oh God, glad to hear your voice, we thought you were dead.” Zoron asked, “How is everyone?” “All ok,” Aura replied, “and we killed all the demons.” “Good job, all of you. Father Rock wants to say something.” Father Rock said, “I’m so proud to have you all as my family. You are all heroes.” Aura said, “Did you kill Demos?” “Not yet,” Zoron said. “We’ve got to go now. Love you, bye." He shut down the mike and checked the screen. "Rockets closing in 10 seconds 9-8-7-6-5-4-3-2-1.” The shield held. “Second hit in 3-2-1, next in 3-2-1,” The shield buckled a little. “Third rocket in 4-3-2-1.” As soon as it hit the shield, Father Rock ordered, “Now hit the super buster shield.” Rockets 4-5-6 hit in one-second intervals: *Boom*! *Boom*! *Boom*! Father Rock was knocked off his chair. He yelled out in pain. Zoron said, “Are you ok?” “I am fine. Give me a damage report.” "One engine at 50% capacity, the rest are good to go,” Zoron said. Father Rock said, “What’s on the screen?” “The Scorpion is closing fast.”

The Scorpion was entering a meteor storm. *Vam*! A meteor hit the Scorpion. *Wap*! Another meteor hit the Scorpion. Great damage was sustained in the navigation control. Dreg said, “One other thing we can try.” Demos said, “What?” He was beating his black fist on the control panel. Smoke was filling the Scorpion. Demos turned to Dreg and said,

"Good bye, you stupid fool." Demos stabbed Dreg through his heart with his long, poisonous fingernails. Dreg's eyes were wide open, watching helplessly as Demos squeezed his heart in his hand. Demos was laughing, roaring. Dreg slumped in his harness, dead. "Now he is out of the way. Father Rock is next." Demos was drunk with power now. He waved his arms in joy. Dreg's blood floated all over the ship. Demos screamed, "I am The Ruler Of The Universe." He keyed the mike and yelled into his radio in his deep, evil voice, "Father Rock, I have killed Dreg, the stupid fool, you're next. Do you receive my message loud and clear?"

Father Rock said, "Zoron, Demos is totally insane. He must be killed now. He would destroy earth just for the fun of it. We have one chance. We must use the cosmic light. Put on the dark glasses to protect your eyes. Ready in five seconds. 5-4-3-2-1," *blast*! The force of the cosmic light was so awesome that Father Rock and Zoron were pressed back in their seats. High frequency sound waves of energy created a vibrating shock that hit the StarFlyer and blew it backward faster than the speed of light. As the StarFlyer shot backward, a deep roar came from within the weaponry and different colored light energy shot out of the front ports. Zoron and Father Rock watched as blue, red, green, and purple light then yellow, pink and white energy formed a protective shield around the StarFlyer. Father Rock said, "It looks like a beautiful rainbow." Father Rock went into a trance and an energy force field formed around his body. He played a mystical sound on his guitar. Zoron had never heard a sound like this before. As Father Rock played the universal cosmic music, Zoron knew that Father Rock was controlling the massive energy force with his mind. Father Rock started playing faster and faster. As he did, electricity surged up and down his body. At the same time, a white energy beam formed in front of the StarFlyer. Father Rock's eyes opened abruptly and white-hot energy beams shot out of his eyes. He shuddered as he played faster and faster. He screamed, "Demos! Demos! I am the light and the sword. I sever your evil energy in the name of God, be gone!" The white energy concentrated into a thin beam and shot through space towards the approaching Scorpion. In an instant, the spacecraft was blown to pieces. The explosion was so bright it looked like a supernova. In the quiet of the aftermath, Father Rock said, "I create all energies, light, matter, vibration and dimensions you see and cannot see. Sound you hear and cannot hear. I am you and you are me. We are all united as one harmonious frequency; from the beginning of time to the now of your existence to infinity.

Demos is dead,
The universe
Is free.
Let us all stand
In the light and
Love of God
In peace.

Eight Months Later

The remnants of the cult gather around the sacrificial table. On the table, a young woman thrashes in the final throes of childbirth. As the child tears his way free, the cult sways and chants, their voices rising to the shrouded ceiling of the musty cave. “Saton, Saton, SATON!” The baby does not cry. His eyes open, disconcertingly black under the innocent fringe of downy red hair. As the chants reach their crescendo, bone-chilling laughter echoes throughout the cavern.

And it begins…

FATHER ROCK

www.ingramcontent.com/pod-product-compliance
Ingram Content Group UK Ltd.
Pitfield, Milton Keynes, MK11 3LW, UK
UKHW041945190726
13854UKWH00004B/1800

9 781425 105754